Praise for

THE SISTERS GRIMM SERIES:

Today Show Kids Book Club Pick
New York Times Bestseller
Book Sense Pick
Oppenheim Toy Portfolio Platinum Award
Kirkus Reviews Best Fantasy Book
A *Real Simple* magazine "Must-Have"
New York Public Library 100 Titles for
    Reading and Sharing Selection

"Why didn't I think of *The Sisters Grimm*?
What a great concept!" —Jane Yolen

"A very fun series . . ." —*Chicago Parent*

★ "The twists and turns of the plot, the clever
humor, and the behind-the-scenes glimpses
of Everafters we think we know will appeal to
many readers." —*Kliatt*, starred review

ALSO BY MICHAEL BUCKLEY:

In the *Sisters Grimm* series:

BOOK ONE: THE FAIRY-TALE DETECTIVES

BOOK TWO: THE UNUSUAL SUSPECTS

BOOK THREE: THE PROBLEM CHILD

BOOK FOUR: ONCE UPON A CRIME

BOOK FIVE: MAGIC AND OTHER MISDEMEANORS

BOOK SIX: TALES FROM THE HOOD

BOOK SEVEN: THE EVERAFTER WAR

BOOK EIGHT: THE INSIDE STORY

BOOK NINE: THE COUNCIL OF MIRRORS

A VERY GRIMM GUIDE

In the *NERDS* series:

BOOK ONE: NATIONAL ESPIONAGE, RESCUE, AND DEFENSE SOCIETY

BOOK TWO: M IS FOR MAMA'S BOY

BOOK THREE: THE CHEERLEADERS OF DOOM

BOOK FOUR: THE VILLAIN VIRUS

THE SISTERS GRIMM

· BOOK FIVE ·

MAGIC AND OTHER MISDEMEANORS

MICHAEL BUCKLEY

PICTURES BY PETER FERGUSON

AMULET BOOKS

New York

PUBLISHER'S NOTE: This is a work of fiction. Names, characters, places, and incidents are either the product of the author's imagination or are used fictitiously, and any resemblance to actual persons, living or dead, business establishments, events, or locales is entirely coincidental.

The Library of Congress has cataloged the hardcover edition as follows:
Buckley, Michael.
Magic and other misdemeanors / by Michael Buckley.
p. cm. — (Sisters Grimm ; bk. 5)
Summary: Fairy-tale detectives Sabrina and Daphne Grimm face their first case without Granny Relda's help when the future gets mixed up with the past in Ferryport Landing, and because some of the future does not look bright, Puck helps them try to make some changes.
ISBN 978-0-8109-9358-7 (alk. paper)
[1. Time—Fiction. 2. Characters in literature—Fiction. 3. Sisters—Fiction. 4. Grandmothers—Fiction. 5. Mystery and detective stories.] I. Title.
PZ7.B882323Mag 2007
[Fic]—dc22
2007029429
Paperback ISBN 978-0-8109-7263-6

Originally published in hardcover by Amulet Books in 2007
Copyright © 2007 Michael Buckley
Illustrations copyright © 2007 Peter Ferguson
Excerpt of *Tales from the Hood* © 2008 Michael Buckley

Printed and bound in U.S.A.
20 19 18 17 16 15 14 13 12 11 10 9

Amulet Books are available at special discounts when purchased in quantity for premiums and promotions as well as fundraising or educational use. Special editions can also be created to specification. For details, contact specialsales@abramsbooks.com or the address below.

THE ART OF BOOKS SINCE 1949
115 West 18th Street
New York, NY 10011
www.abramsbooks.com

For Alison. You put a spell on me.

ACKNOWLEDGMENTS

Many thanks to my editor, Susan Van Metre, whose insight and hard work continues to make this a great series. Special thanks to Maggie Lehrman for her careful editing and extraordinary ideas; Jason Wells at Amulet for making me famous and keeping me on time; my wife and literary agent, Alison Fargis, who's willing to be the bad guy when I'm too much of a coward. A big thanks to Joe Deasy, who continues to read these stories over and over and give me great advice. Thanks to my Pacific Northwest cheerleader, Stefanie Frank, as well as Ms. Mock and her class at Hammond Hill Elementary. Big shout-outs to Mark Rifkin and Ellen Scordato for their many big shout-outs. And a very special thank you to Donald Scherschligt and his wonderful family. I eagerly await Donald's first novel and the day I can say, I knew him when.

THE SISTERS GRIMM

BOOK FIVE

MAGIC AND OTHER MISDEMEANORS

PUCK FLAPPED HIS WINGS HARD, *but nothing he did could stop his body from being pulled toward the black, gaping hole that hovered above him. He looked like a worm struggling to avoid the hungry jaws of a catfish.*

"Hello! We've got a problem," he cried as he flailed in midair.

Sabrina did the only thing she could think to do. She grabbed Puck's foot as he sailed past, hoping that their combined weight would stop his drift. Unfortunately she, too, was jerked off the ground. She cried out, but her grandmother, uncle, and Mr. Canis were too far away to reach her. Only Sabrina's sister, Daphne, was nearby. The little girl latched onto Sabrina's pant leg and was yanked off the ground as well. Now all three of them were caught in the hole's swirling gravitational pull.

Puck's face passed through the black hole and his head disappeared. His upper torso and arms followed, then his waist, and finally his knees. All that was left in this world of the boy fairy were his sneakers. Sabrina clung to them with all her strength, attempting to defy the impossible force.

"We're losing him," Daphne cried desperately.

"Puck, you have to fight it!" Sabrina shouted.

But her own words sounded laughable in Sabrina's ears. How could he fight something with such a powerful hunger? What could any of them do to stop themselves, and soon the rest of the world, from being sucked into nothingness?

Puck's shoes disappeared into the hole, though Sabrina could still feel them. She knew if she let go he would be gone forever, but she had problems of her own. The hole was starting to swallow her up. Both her arms sunk into the empty, dark pool. She took a deep breath and said a final silent prayer for her soul, hoping that God would find her on the other side, wherever that might be.

And then the hole quadrupled in size.

1

I'm sure this could be seen as child abuse," Sabrina groaned as she pulled a pillow over her head. She wondered how many children had grandmothers who woke them up by standing over their beds banging a metal pot with a spoon. She peeked out at the old woman. Granny Relda looked like a member of the world's most annoying marching band.

"Up and at 'em!" Granny cried as she continued her obnoxious drumming. Granny Relda was fully dressed, wearing a bulky coat, mittens, a scarf, and boots. She might have looked as if she were going whale hunting if not for her bright pink hat with the sunflower appliqué in its center.

"I'm up," Sabrina said.

"Sorry, *liebling*," Granny replied in her light German accent. "But this is the only way to wake your sister."

Sabrina rolled over and eyed her seven-year-old sister, Daphne. The two of them had shared a bed for some time now and she was well aware of how soundly Daphne slept. The little girl could doze through a class-five hurricane, so Granny had resorted to finding the loudest, most ear-shattering methods to rouse the little girl. In an effort to save her own eardrums, Sabrina vigorously shook her little sister until Daphne's eyes opened.

"Whazzamattawitallthebangin?" she grumbled.

"It's time to start the day," Granny said, finally setting down her pot and spoon. "We've got to get in a little escape training before everyone arrives."

Both the girls groaned.

"Granny, we hate escape training. We're no good at it," Daphne complained.

"Nonsense," the old woman said, helping the girls out of bed. "You're both very good at it."

"Then how come we've never escaped?" Sabrina grumbled.

Granny did her best to hide her smile. "Get dressed, girls. Like I said, we have a big day and there is no time for dilly-dallying."

"What do we wear?" Sabrina said, crossing the room and opening the closet door.

"Dress warmly," Granny said as she left the room. "Dress very, very warmly."

The girls dressed as quickly as their tired bodies would allow. They had come to understand their grandmother and knew to prepare accordingly. If she said to dress lightly, that meant shorts and T-shirts. If she said bring a towel, that meant bring a dozen. If she said dress warmly, that meant two pairs of long-johns, four pairs of socks, heavy blue jeans, boots, two sweaters, scarves, mittens, and a down coat. Very, very warmly might well mean bringing along a portable space heater. Sabrina added a little wooden sword to her ensemble, shoving it into her coat pocket.

"What's that for?" Daphne asked, eyeing the weapon.

"You never know," Sabrina said, and she and Daphne went to join Granny Relda.

The old house was a museum of memories. Every wall was decorated with photographs from Granny Relda and Grandpa Basil's months of honeymoon adventures. Sabrina saw a picture of the two of them holding an enormous fish near an icy river, another of them white-water rafting, and still another posing in what appeared to be Red Square. There were many more photos of the girls and their father and mother. There was even one wall dedicated to the family dog, Elvis.

Their uncle Jake stepped out of the bathroom as they went down the hallway. He was a handsome blond man, a bit on the lanky side, with a crooked nose he had gotten in a fistfight. He was still in his pajamas and had a toothbrush in his mouth.

"Good luck," he said, giving them a thumbs-up gesture.

"Easy for you to say," Sabrina mumbled. "You don't have to spend your mornings running from a certifiable psychopath."

"You say it like it's not going to be any fun," Uncle Jake said with a grin.

Granny met them at a door at the end of the hall. She reached into her ever-present handbag and took out a giant key ring. There must have been a hundred keys—made of gold, silver, crystal, brass—on the ring. There was even a skeleton key that looked as if it had been made from a real skeleton. Granny sorted through the keys, found the one she wanted, and then inserted it into the door. When it was open, she escorted the girls inside. There, Sabrina found herself in a spare bedroom with an ornate, full-length mirror hanging on the wall and a queen-size bed in the middle of the room. On the bed were her parents, Henry and Veronica Grimm. They were sound asleep, as they had been for the last several months.

"Go on, girls," Granny said, nudging them forward.

Sabrina and Daphne walked up to the mirror. Daphne reached out to touch its surface and her hand slid through. The reflection rippled and moved like water upset by a skipping stone. Then she did something most people would have thought impossible: She stepped through the reflection and vanished. Sabrina and her grandmother followed.

The group found themselves in a brilliantly lit hallway, as big as Grand Central Station, with enormous columns holding up a barreled ceiling. The hall seemed to go on forever and was lined on both sides by doors. A little man in a black tuxedo was waiting for the Grimms. He had thinning hair and a soft, kind face.

"Look at my little snow bunnies," the man said as he clapped his hands with glee.

"Hello, Mirror," Sabrina said.

"Are you ready for the escape training?" Mirror asked. He gave her a wink for encouragement.

Daphne grumbled something under her breath.

"They're both a little tired," Granny explained.

"Well, I suppose we should get started," Mirror said as he turned and led the group down the hall. Sabrina looked at the doors on both sides. Some were made from wood, some steel, and others from more unusual substances. Once she had seen one that seemed to be made out of fire. Each door had a little brass plaque that stated the contents of the room beyond: magic carpets, unicorns, enchanted armor, golden fleeces, lions, witches, wardrobes—the rooms went on and on.

Finally, the group stopped at a door with a little plaque that read "The Snow Queen's Homeland." Granny handed Mirror her keys and he went to work unlocking the door.

"Hey, wait a minute. I've read the story of the Snow Queen," Sabrina said.

"Indeed," Granny said. "Hans Christian Andersen wrote about her."

"Yeah, and he said she was a nutcase and a killer. She froze some poor kid to death!"

"Are we going to be safe?" Daphne asked.

"The Snow Queen doesn't live here anymore, girls," Granny explained. "This is just where she was born. Now she lives on Beechwood Avenue near Old McDonald's farm. I think she drives an ice-cream truck. All right, girls. Let's get started."

The door opened and bitter cold wind blasted the group. Sabrina swore she could feel icicles forming on her back teeth. She looked up at her grandmother. "Are you crazy?"

"This is going to be fun," the old woman shouted over the noise as she stepped inside.

"Good luck! See you when you get back," Mirror said as he nudged the girls through and closed the door.

Sabrina glanced around. She had learned that some of the rooms held magical items and others held unusual creatures, but only recently had she discovered that some of the rooms led to other worlds. They'd been to the top of a Mist Giant's mountain, on an island that seemed to be alive, and inside a volcano—all inhospitable. But this world, this Snow Queen's Homeland, was the worst. Everything was covered in ice. There were huge boulders of it wherever she looked. The frost-encrusted ground was rock hard. Even the forest that stretched out before them was frozen stiff.

"My eyelids are sticking together," Daphne said as she rubbed her eyes.

"Go on, girls," Granny said, pointing to a path that led up a hill bordering a dark wood. "You know how this works. Walk ahead. When you hear my whistle, you'll know you've gone far enough. Then turn around and try to make it back to me. Easy as pie!"

Sabrina knew arguing was pointless, so she took her sister by the hand and started down the path. They hadn't gone more than a few yards when they heard laughter echoing through the woods.

"He knows we're here," Sabrina said.

"This is all your fault," Daphne replied.

"My fault?" Sabrina cried. "How is this my fault?"

"You called him an ugly freak baby at dinner last night. Now he's out for revenge."

"It was a term of endearment."

"Well, he's going to make this extra hard on us today."

After a while, the girls heard their grandmother's whistle.

"There it is," Sabrina said. "Time to head back."

They stopped, looked around, and started back down the path. A moment later they heard more laughter and the sound of flapping wings.

"The ugly freak baby is on his way," Daphne said.

The ugly freak baby in question was named Puck. He was a four-thousand-year-old fairy who looked like an eleven-year-old boy but acted much younger. The Trickster King, as he called himself, was a master of obnoxious pranks, vulgar manners, and dirty tricks. He was also the bane of Sabrina's existence. He had taken a particular interest in humiliating her whenever possible, which was most of the time. Unfortunately, Granny Relda felt Puck was the right person to help the girls think on their feet and escape from unpredictable situations. So he had become a sort of teacher to them as they trained for their futures as full-fledged detectives. Unfortunately, his teaching strategy was somewhat disturbing, so now when they heard a loud explosion on the path next to them, they knew that school was in session.

Frightened, they darted behind an enormous snow-covered tree and peered around the trunk. Puck was nowhere in sight, but they could hear the beating of his wings over the chill wind.

"Puck booby-trapped the path," Daphne said, shivering. "We should head for the forest."

Sabrina peered at a bank of fir trees several yards off the path. They were thick and would make good cover, but Sabrina was sick of hiding. Puck always caught them in the woods. He could fly over and see where they were. It wasn't fair.

"He's expecting us to run into the woods. We do it every time."

"Hiding is good," Daphne said. "I'm a big fan of hiding."

"I bet that first explosion is the only one on the path. Why would he booby-trap the rest of it if he assumes we're going to hide in the forest?"

"Then what should we do?"

Sabrina furrowed her brow and thought, searching through her mental filing cabinet from her year and a half in foster care. Puck wasn't the only clever one in the Grimm household. Sabrina could get in and out of a house undetected, pick a few simple locks, and run like the wind before anyone knew she was gone. Puck might have called himself the Trickster King, but Sabrina had a name for herself—the Queen of the Sneaks.

"Let's just stay on the path and run real fast," Sabrina said.

Daphne's face crinkled as if she'd bitten into a sour pickle. "You want to stay in the open?"

"And run real fast," Sabrina repeated.

"What if you're wrong?" Daphne asked.

"Then Granny Relda is going to wake us up early again tomorrow," Sabrina said. "It's worth a shot."

Daphne peeked around the corner, then turned back to her sister. "I don't know about—"

But Sabrina didn't give her sister time to think about the plan. She snatched her by the hand and dragged her back to the path, which led down a slight hill lined with pricker bushes. Each icy thorn sparkled like jagged glass, so they went slowly and paid attention to their steps. Sabrina's plan seemed to be working. They hadn't set off another booby trap. Could they have actually out-tricked the Trickster King?

Soon they came across a chunk of ice as big as a car. They stopped to catch their breaths and hid behind it with their backs pressed against its chilly surface. Sabrina took the opportunity to make sure the little wooden sword was still in her pocket.

"I think we did it," Daphne said, peeking around the boulder. "You're mucho smart-o."

"Mucho smart-o?"

"It's my new word," Daphne said. "It means you're very smart."

"In what language?"

"Daphne-ish," the little girl said matter-of-factly. Sabrina's sister was always coming up with odd little words or sayings. No one had any idea where any of them came from, but Daphne seemed to have a new one each week.

"You're really good at thinking on your feet. I wish I was better at it," the little girl continued.

"Well, you're very good at the magic stuff. I wish I could use a wand," Sabrina said ruefully. "I guess I'll do what I'm good at, and you'll do what you're good at."

"We make a pretty good team," Daphne said, hugging her sister.

"We do," Sabrina agreed.

"Isn't this just the sweetest moment ever?" a familiar voice said from above, followed by a mischievous snicker. "I'm going to get a cavity."

"Puck," Daphne groaned.

Sabrina craned her neck to get a good look at the boy. He

was standing on top of the ice boulder. He wore a grungy green hoodie and jeans covered in mud, food, and heaven only knew what else. He had a shaggy head of hair, dazzling blue eyes, and a devilish smirk on his face. His pink-streaked insect wings fluttered behind him and he held a coconut-shaped device that looked a lot like a grenade. He had half a dozen more of them strapped across his chest.

"What's that in your hand, Puck?" Sabrina asked suspiciously.

"It's my latest creation. I call it a glop grenade. Allow me to demonstrate," Puck said. "All you do is pull the pin, count to three, and throw it. The unfortunate moron in its path is sprayed with all manner of disgusting rubbish. This one is filled with fur balls and chili. You're going to have to take a lot of showers to wash this off. You'll probably have to burn your clothes, too. So where was I? Oh yes, one . . ."

Sabrina lifted her hands to show him they were clenched into fists. "You throw that thing at us, and it will be the biggest mistake of your miserable life, fairy boy."

"Two," Puck continued, unimpressed.

Sabrina watched him wind up to throw the grenade, and with reflexes faster than she even suspected she possessed, she snatched her little sword from her coat pocket and brought it down on his hand. He cried out and dropped the device. It hit the ground and rolled toward a tree, exploding an icky brown-and-yellow slime all over the bark. The frigid air quickly hardened the substance into an icy shell. Unfortunately, the air couldn't freeze the revolting aroma that wafted into Sabrina's nose. She almost gagged.

"You're going to pay for that, snotface," Puck snarled, but Sabrina was no fool. She was already on her feet and pulling Daphne down the path.

"Look at the piggies run!" she heard him cry. "Silly piggies! You can't outrun me."

He was probably right, but she was going to try anyway. She ran as fast as she could, stumbling along as she lost her footing over and over again on the slippery terrain. Daphne was having just as much difficulty.

"One! Two! Three!" she heard Puck shout, and another foul-smelling explosion splattered the ground just inches away. Luckily, Daphne pulled Sabrina back in the nick of time.

"C'mon!" The little girl shouted as she fled from the path and into the forest.

"No! That's what he wants us to do!" Sabrina cried.

"We don't have any other choice," Daphne said as another glop grenade exploded onto the tree next to them.

They ran through an outcropping of tightly packed frozen

maples. Sabrina hoped the trees would provide the girls with cover for a moment so she could think about what to do next. But her hopes were dashed when she spotted the trees' inhabitants. Hiding in the branches above the girls' heads was an army of chimpanzees dressed in white-and-gray camouflage overalls and wearing matching soldiers' helmets. Each chimp was holding one of Puck's glop grenades in its long, furry hands. The sight of them brought the sisters to a screeching halt.

"OK. No sudden movements," Sabrina said, recalling her first encounter with Puck's primate privates. They were a nasty bunch, but if the girls were careful, they might get away from them. "Just be quiet and take a slow step backward."

Daphne did as she was told while Sabrina kept an eye on the chimps. The beasts made no motion to attack. They just stared at the girls with a dull curiosity.

"They're going to let us go," Daphne said. "They're nice monkeys."

Sabrina cringed when she heard the first angry shriek. Before she knew it, all the chimps were gnashing their teeth and jumping up and down in the branches.

"What's wrong?" Daphne said.

"They're not monkeys! They're chimpanzees, and they're very

sensitive about it," Sabrina explained as the first of the grenades exploded at their feet, splattering the ground in what looked like brown gravy and mayonnaise. "We should run."

But Daphne was already running back the way she came.

"Traitor!" Sabrina shouted, chasing after her. Unfortunately, the chimps were in hot pursuit. They swung from limb to limb, screaming and spitting and tossing their disgusting weapons at the girls. Explosions went off all around them, and the best the girls could do was cover their heads, run, and hope for the best.

"This is so stupid," Daphne cried. "If I had the Shoes of Swiftness, we'd be out of here in a flash. I could even stop this with the Golden Cap. I'd like to see their little faces when a wave of flying monkeys came at them. Doing this without magic is mucho lame-o!"

"Just head back to the path," Sabrina said. She could see the trees were thinning out, leaving the primates fewer branches to swing from. It wasn't long before the dirty fur balls were tumbling out of the trees and falling into the huge snowdrifts below. Those that didn't fall must have heard the others' painful thuds and were smart enough to give up the chase. Sabrina glanced back and saw them shake their fists at her and her sister.

Once the girls were back on the path, they found themselves

at the top of another steep embankment. At its bottom Sabrina spotted a thin black ribbon of smoke rising into the air. She looked for the source: a small fire burning at the bottom of the hill. Sabrina squinted and saw Granny Relda sitting next to it in a Victorian-style stuffed chair, with her legs propped up on an ottoman. Sabrina couldn't help but grin, especially when the woman rose to her feet and waved at them. Granny Relda had never seen them get so close, and judging by her reaction, she was elated. A wave of pride rolled over Sabrina.

"Let's go before—"

Sabrina didn't get to finish her sentence. Gravity and the icy ground sent her flailing down the hill. She'd grabbed Daphne's arm on her way down, hoping it would stop her, but all it did was yank her little sister off her feet. Together they went sliding down the embankment.

"No fair!" Puck cried as he swooped down over them. He tossed another grenade, then another and another, but none landed close enough to cause any damage. Not that the girls were doing anything to avoid his attack. They were spinning, flopping, skidding, tumbling, and careening down the hill with no way to steer or stop. When they reached the bottom, they slammed into their grandmother.

"*Lieblings!* Are you OK?" Granny Relda asked. The old woman

had fallen on her back and was struggling like a turtle to right herself.

"We're fine, Granny," Daphne replied. "Are you hurt?"

Granny Relda smiled as Sabrina helped her to her feet. "I'm fine. Congratulations. You passed the test!"

Suddenly, Puck appeared overhead with his last grenade in hand.

"No way! You cheated, stinkpot!" Puck cried.

"How did we cheat?" Daphne said.

"I don't know yet," Puck said, tossing the last of his weapons. It hit the ground and rolled in between Sabrina's legs.

"Puck, NO! The girls beat you!" Granny shouted as she threw up her arms and backed away.

Sabrina cringed and prepared to be drenched in something disgusting. After a few moments, she opened her eyes and studied Puck's weapon. There was something different about this one. Something was there that shouldn't have been. Sabrina smiled. The pin was still inserted.

"Uh-oh," Puck said.

"One," Sabrina said as she pulled the pin.

"Put it down, piggy!" Puck cried.

"Two," Sabrina said.

"I'm warning you. I'll make you regret it."

Sabrina didn't wait for three. She threw the grenade. It hit Puck in the chest and exploded into a wave of purple nastiness that smelled like rotten eggs, pumpkins, and ranch dressing. The substance soaked him all over and then froze instantly in the chilly air, enclosing him in an icy cocoon. His big pink wings were the only things not trapped. They flapped furiously, but the added weight of ice was too much, and he plummeted to the ground with a thud.

Granny went to him and rested her hand on his frozen head. "We'll get you out lickety-split," she said to him, then turned to the girls and gestured behind the chair. There was a door, standing by itself in open space. "Go ahead, *lieblings*. You earned it."

Sabrina and Daphne approached the door. Together they clenched the doorknob in their hands and turned it. The door opened, flooding them in warm air and bright light. Sabrina turned to her sister and caught her beaming smile. She took Daphne's hand and together they stepped through the doorway.

Mirror and Uncle Jake were waiting on the other side.

"So, what's the verdict?" Uncle Jake asked.

Daphne smiled even harder. "We passed!"

"Congrats, peanut," Uncle Jake cried, swooping her up in his arms. He planted a big smooch on the little girl's forehead. "I knew you could do it."

Mirror rushed to Sabrina and shook her hand vigorously. "Well done!"

"Thank you, Mirror," Sabrina said. She could feel her chest swelling up with pride. It was unusual for her family to praise her—not that she could blame them. In the past she had been a cranky, argumentative jerk.

A third man joined the celebration, approaching from the mirror's portal at the end of the hall. He was enormous, standing nearly seven feet tall, with a shock of gray hair and bright gray eyes. His hands, one of which had dark black talons, were covered in fur and he had a bushy tail. He also looked very tired.

"Mr. Canis," Granny said. "The girls passed their escape test."

"I am pleased," Mr. Canis said, though his face didn't reflect his words. The old man did not smile often. "Some of the guests have arrived."

"Oh, dear me," Granny cried. "I'm not even finished cooking—oh, and Puck! Oh dear, Jacob, he could use a hand. He's just on the other side of the door. He can't move."

Uncle Jake stepped through the doorway. A moment later he returned with Puck hoisted on his shoulder, still frozen solid.

"Where should I put him?" Jake asked, smelling the boy. "Oh, mercy! He smells like a septic tank."

"Put him in the shower," Granny said. "The hot water will melt the ice and he could use a bath anyway."

Puck made an angry mumble. Bathing was not one of his favorite pastimes.

"Stop your grumbling," Granny said to the boy. "When you're out of the shower, I'd like you to wear something clean. Perhaps that blue shirt with the cute little alligator on it that I bought for you."

Puck's unpleasant mumbling got louder.

"Puck! Wear the shirt!" Granny Relda insisted. "We're having guests."

Daphne's face sprouted an ecstatic smile and she clapped her hands like a child at a birthday party. "The princesses are coming!"

"If you don't need anything, Relda, I believe I'll retire to my room," Mr. Canis said.

"You don't want to join us, old friend?" Granny Relda asked.

Mr. Canis shook his head and shuffled back down the long hallway. He hadn't always been a hairy giant. When the girls had first met him, he seemed like the skinniest old man in the world, but he was changing, and not for the better. His new appearance reminded people that he had a monster called the Big Bad Wolf trapped inside him that was slowly clawing its way out.

The group walked along the hallway to the portal that led back into the real world. They stepped through it into the spare bedroom where Henry and Veronica rested. Uncle Jake carried Puck to the shower while Granny and Daphne rushed off to greet the guests arriving downstairs. Sabrina, however, lingered, sitting down on the bed next to her parents. Henry and Veronica lay quietly, as if they were enjoying an afternoon nap. Sabrina ran her hand across her father's stubbly beard and kissed her mother on the forehead. So far, the family hadn't found anything that could break the spell that kept her parents asleep. Sometimes, in the still of night, Sabrina would wake up in a panic, convinced her parents were somehow conscious, feeling helpless and abandoned. She would creep out of bed and spend an hour or two looking over them, assuring them that she was working as hard as she could on a remedy for their enchanted slumber.

A normal person would have probably been very disturbed by what Sabrina had just seen—a boy with wings, magical doorways, glop grenades, a wolfman, parents trapped under magic spells—but for Sabrina Grimm, it was just another day in Ferryport Landing.

She hadn't always spent her afternoons in such odd surroundings. She had once been a normal girl living in New York City with her little sister, Daphne, and her parents. She remembered there had actually been times when she thought her family was boring. That all changed the night Henry and Veronica disappeared. The police searched high and low for them and found only one clue—the abandoned family car, with a bloodred handprint painted on the dashboard. With no known next of kin, the girls were dumped into an orphanage and then into the foster-care system, where they spent a year and a half bouncing from one certifiable lunatic to the next. They'd lived with paranoid schizophrenics, mean-spirited kids, angry animals, and every other weirdo the state would grant a child.

When they were sent to live with their grandmother, Sabrina was sure the old woman was just another whack-a-doodle. After all, Sabrina and Daphne's grandmother was supposed to be dead. Their father had told them this himself. Of course "Granny Relda," as they eventually called her, didn't help her case much. She had a lot of crazy stories, including one in which the girls were the youngest living descendents of Jacob and Wilhelm Grimm—also known as the Brothers Grimm. Granny Relda said the brothers' famous book of fairy tales was actually a history of true events. Along with other writing legends like L. Frank Baum, Rudyard Kipling, and Hans Christian Andersen, they had documented what they witnessed in order to warn the world about magical phenomena. In fact, she claimed, most of these storybook characters, who now preferred to be called Everafters, still lived in their new hometown, Ferryport Landing.

That was the good news. The bad news was every Everafter in town was stuck there—trapped inside a magical bubble set up by their great-great-great-great-great-grandfather Wilhelm Grimm to prevent a war between humans and fairy-tale folk. Worse still, a lot of the Everafters deeply resented their imprisonment and many directed their anger toward the Grimm family.

Naturally, Sabrina thought the old woman was off her rocker. Until Granny Relda was kidnapped by a giant.

The girls rescued her and were soon caught up in the fight to stop other deranged Everafters from destroying the town. They discovered that all the bad guys they came across had one thing in common: They were members of a shadowy group known as the Scarlet Hand. No one knew how many Everafters were members or who their mysterious "Master" was, but one thing was for sure—the Scarlet Hand planned on taking over the world.

Sabrina had fought her destiny for a long time. She wasn't interested in becoming a fairy-tale detective like her father, grandmother, and everyone before them, even though her sister embraced the job. For Sabrina, the danger, chaos, and just plain craziness of the family occupation had taken some getting used to. Only recently, after a trip to New York City, had Sabrina realized that there were many ways to be a Grimm. She also realized it was time for her to give the family business a chance.

Unfortunately, avoiding a glop grenade wielded by a mischievous flying boy was part of the package. Sabrina and Daphne's days were packed with training: lessons on clue finding, self-defense, crime-scene investigation, tracking, and the use of magical items. The latter was a class Daphne excelled in, primarily because Sabrina didn't feel right around too much magic. She had learned that she didn't like who she became when she used it—she was addicted, or "touched" as some of the Everafters said. Still, Granny felt it might be useful if Sabrina understood how magic worked and, more important, how she might defend herself and her sister against it. The training never ended and the pace was exhausting. But Sabrina was secretly enjoying herself—especially when it came to things she excelled at, like tracking and self-defense. She was a natural at clue finding, and she enjoyed criminal psychology, taught by former police deputies Boarman and Swineheart. That's where the girls learned that thinking like criminals helped you catch them. All of it was fun . . . except for the glop grenades, of course.

As Sabrina sat on the bed she spotted a large, bulbous head with thick, muscular features in the ornate mirror she and her family had just stepped through. Mirror's face looked very different when he was peering out at them. He could seem intimidating, almost frightening. Sabrina supposed this face was to protect the secrets that were hidden on the other side of the reflection.

"How are the sleepyheads?" he asked.

"The same," Sabrina said with a sigh.

"Well, that's what the party is for. Maybe someone will have the key to waking them up."

Sabrina nodded hopefully. "Granny asked everyone that's ever been enchanted over tonight. Daphne is nearly jumping out of her pants. She's in a princess phase."

"All little girls have them," Mirror said with a smile.

"Not me," Sabrina said.

Mirror chuckled. "Of course not. You're rough and tough."

"You bet I am," she said, ignoring his teasing. Mirror had become a good friend since she and her sister had moved in with their grandmother. Unlike other enchanted items, the magic mirror was also a person—flesh and blood, though he couldn't leave the confines of the great hall inside his reflection. He had become a confidant to Sabrina, and she turned to him more than anyone else. He always seemed to understand how she felt.

"By the way, you haven't told me what you want for your birthday yet. It's four days away," he said. "It's not easy to shop when you're trapped inside a mirror. My computer is still on dial-up."

"The only thing I want is to find a way to wake them up," Sabrina said, looking at her parents.

Mirror shook his head pityingly. "It'll happen, sugarplum. Now, you better get downstairs. I hear people arriving, and you've got to keep an eye on your uncle. He's also going through a princess phase, from what I'm told."

Sabrina laughed. "That's Uncle Jake. He's girl-crazy."

Mirror's head faded from the reflection. Sabrina leaned over, kissed her mom and dad each on the cheek, and got up from the bed. "We're going to wake you up," she told them. "I promise."

2

he house was filled with guests, most of whom were very unusual. Among the crowd were witches, princesses, a dwarf, and a few knights of the round table. Everyone was munching on snacks and drinking punch.

In one corner Sabrina saw a trio of women known as the Three. They were a coven of witches who used to work for the former mayor of Ferryport Landing. They used magic to cover up things the Everafters didn't want the town's human population to see. One of the women was Glinda the Good Witch, whose life was chronicled in L. Frank Baum's *The Wizard of Oz*. She wore an emerald green pantsuit and held a wand with a crystal star on its end. The second woman looked like she was a million years old. Her name was Frau Pfefferkuchenhaus, otherwise known as the witch from the Hansel and Gretel story. Rounding out the group was the exotic and beautiful Morgan le Fay, famous for her part in the story of King Arthur. The Three were enjoying some crackers and soft cheeses while talking about something that had happened on a televised dancing contest.

In another corner was a diminutive man in a black suit whom Sabrina had met on many occasions. Mr. Seven, as he was called, was better known as one of the seven dwarfs. Like the Three, he used to work for the mayor. Mr. Seven ate from a tray of green cookies set out on the dining room table. As Sabrina watched him, she felt something about him was different. It took a minute to realize that he wasn't wearing the dunce hat his former boss had always made him wear.

Sabrina turned her attention to Daphne, who was sitting on the family's sofa wearing a shiny sequined tiara. Elvis, the family's two-hundred-pound Great Dane, lay on the floor, resting his massive head in Daphne's lap. Snow White sat next to them. Looking at the beautiful woman was like looking at the sunrise for too long. Ms. White was tall and lean with skin like porcelain and eyes as blue as the sky. Sabrina wondered how many car accidents Ms. White had inadvertently caused when drivers took their eyes off the road to catch a glimpse of her walking down the street. Besides her incredible looks, Ms. White was a kind and caring person, as well as an expert in judo, karate, kickboxing, and bow-staff fighting. She came to the Grimm house three times a week to train the girls in self-defense. Like Mr. Seven and the Three, Ms. White was out of work, so she had plenty of free time. Ever since the new mayor took office, the school where she used to teach had been closed, and there was no news of when it would reopen.

Unfortunately, the last three months had not been easy for Snow White. In addition to being unemployed, she was also suffering from a broken heart. After she reconciled with her former fiancé, Prince Charming, the couple looked as if they were headed down the aisle at last. But Charming had disappeared after he lost his re-election bid for mayor. Granny and the girls had searched high and low for him, but it was as if William "Billy" Charming had ceased to exist. Ms. White was upset, but now she seemed particularly distraught.

"Hello, Ms. White," Sabrina said.

"Huh? Oh, I'm sorry, Sabrina. Did you say something?" Ms. White asked.

"She's a little freaked out," Daphne said, pointing across the room.

Sabrina turned and spotted another breathtaking woman standing with two plump fairy godmothers. Her name was Briar Rose, though most knew her as Sleeping Beauty. She had a dark honey complexion and eyes like hot chocolate. Her ever-present smile was soft and she was a bit shy. She had been visiting the family a lot lately. Uncle Jake had asked her for help finding a cure for Henry and Veronica, and Ms. Rose said she was happy to try. Sabrina knew her uncle had a crazy crush on the princess, but unfortunately, Ms. Rose never went anywhere without her overprotective fairy godmothers, Buzzflower and Mallobarb. The fairy duo had made it clear to Uncle Jake that they would not allow Briar to date him until he cut his hair and became royalty. Sabrina knew there was little chance of either happening.

"Why? What's wrong with Ms. Rose?" Sabrina asked her sister.

"Charming used to be married to her," Daphne whispered.

"Awkward," Sabrina whispered back.

"I think I need some wine. Who wants some wine?" Snow White offered as she got to her feet.

"Um, I'm seven," Daphne said.

"Of course you are," Snow White said, walking toward the kitchen.

Uncle Jake strutted into the room and over to Ms. Rose. At once Buzzflower and Mallobarb stepped between them, blocking Jake as if they were linebackers protecting a star quarterback.

"Poor Uncle Jake," Sabrina said.

"He's got the googly eyes for Briar," Daphne replied as she gave Elvis's ears a good scratching. The big dog's back leg tapped the floor happily. "You know what? I think we need to find Elvis a girlfriend."

Elvis snorted, got up with a grunt, and skulked out of the room.

"What did I say?" Daphne cried.

"I guess he's a bachelor," Sabrina said.

Someone knocked on the door, and Granny rushed through the room to answer it. Sabrina and Daphne watched as a sun-soaked blond woman and an elderly man with a cane entered the house. Sabrina didn't recognize either of them.

"Cindy! Tom! What a pleasant surprise. Please come in," Granny said. "Let me take your jackets."

Cindy was another rare beauty. She had a button nose and high, freckled cheekbones and a smile so bright it seemed to block out the rest of her face. Tom, on the other hand, was well into his eighties, with a gaunt face and shaking hands. He leaned on his long brown cane and held a leather satchel close to his body. He wore a tweed jacket and an old-fashioned felt hat.

"I hope we're not intruding," Cindy said.

"I heard about the get-together and I insisted we come over. I thought we might be able to help," Tom offered.

"The more the merrier," Granny said cheerfully.

"And if we can't help, at least we can do the dishes at the end of the night," Tom said as he set his bag on the floor near the couch.

"Cindy, Tom, I think you know everyone here but my granddaughters," Granny Relda said, gesturing at the girls. "Sabrina, Daphne, this is Mr. Baxter and his wife, Dr. Baxter."

"Are you Everafters?" Daphne said, shaking the old man's hand.

Tom laughed. "Alas no, but my wife falls into that category."

Daphne cocked her eyebrow and gazed at the woman.

"I'm Cinderella," Cindy said as if slightly embarrassed.

Daphne let out a squeal so loud that everyone in the house fell silent. Even Elvis rushed back into the room and looked around wildly.

"Sorry," Sabrina said to the crowd. "She was dropped on her head when she was little."

Daphne inserted the palm of her hand into her mouth and bit down on it. It was one of the odd quirks she displayed when she was excited or happy or both.

"Yobubbaingalllah," Daphne said.

"Pardon?" Cindy said.

Daphne removed her palm. "I'm so excited I might barf!"

Cindy smiled. "It's very nice to meet you girls. Your father was—I mean, is—one of my favorite people."

"He has such a kind spirit," Tom added.

"We're big fans too," Sabrina said, shaking the man's hand.

"Cindy hosts a radio show here in town," Granny explained. "Or should I be calling you Dr. Cindy?"

"Cindy's fine," the woman said with a laugh.

"We've got good news. We're about to go national," Tom said proudly. "Soon *The Dr. Cindy Show* will be giving advice to people all over the country."

"What kind of advice?" Sabrina asked.

"My specialty is family issues," Cindy replied. "I had a bit of a rough childhood, and I use my experiences to help families get along."

Elvis trotted over to the old man's bag, sniffed it, and let out a whine. Granny grabbed him by the collar and pulled him away. "Elvis, behave," she said. The dog let out a little grunt but did as he was told.

While Granny put Elvis in the kitchen, Sabrina watched the old man slip his hand into his wife's. He looked at her the way someone looks at a beautiful waterfall. Sabrina had seen that look on her parents' faces and in the photographs of her grandmother and grandfather. Cindy looked back at her husband with the same expression. *They've got the googly eyes,* Sabrina thought.

Puck made his entrance in typical fashion. He stepped into the middle of the room and let out a tremendous belch. "I'm here!" he shouted, as if the crowd had been waiting for his arrival. When no one responded, he turned to Sabrina.

"I'm not a happy camper. I look like a fool," he said. He was wearing the shirt Granny Relda had asked him to wear. It had a little happy alligator on it, but Puck had taken a magic marker and written I EAT PEOPLE in a talk balloon above its head.

"It's a nice shirt," Sabrina said, trying to cheer the boy up.

Puck sneered. "'It's a nice shirt,'" he mocked. "I am the most diabolical villain in the history of the world. I have caused chaos and disaster everywhere I have gone. I have brought nations to their knees. I can't be seen in this shirt. For one, the alligator is smiling. If you wish me to wear a shirt with a man-eating beast on it, the beast should be eating a man, or at least a bear or something equally vicious. This alligator looks as if it's ready for some birthday cake. If Jonas the Betrayer saw me, I would never live it down."

"Jonas the Betrayer?" Daphne asked.

Sabrina shrugged.

"Well, I think we are all here," Granny said before Puck could continue his tirade. She stood in the center of the living room and called for everyone's attention. "I appreciate each one of you for taking the time to come and offer your suggestions for our dilemma. I know that you are all very busy, and it's not exactly a good time to be talking to a Grimm."

"Mayor Heart isn't going to tell us who we can talk to," Morgan le Fay said.

The crowd murmured in agreement.

"Thank you," Granny said. "As you all know, my family has a reputation as problem-solvers. Many of you have come to us for help. Now, we have a problem and we are turning to you. Tonight I'm asking you to put your heads together and find a way around the spell keeping my son and his wife asleep."

Just then, there was another knock at the door.

"Oh, a late arrival. Sabrina, could you answer that for me?" Granny asked.

Sabrina hurried to the door, not wanting to miss a second of the meeting. She threw the door open but nearly fell backward when she saw who was waiting on the other side. A decrepit old woman dressed in filthy rags peered at her through bushy white eyebrows. She smelled of death. Behind her a rundown shack resting on top of two enormous chicken legs paced back and forth around the family's yard.

"Baba Yaga!" Sabrina gasped.

The old crone eyed Sabrina with a hot and angry stare. Every wrinkle, wart, and scar seemed to convey the witch's bitter hatred.

"I was invited," she growled as she pushed past Sabrina to enter the house. A fold of Baba Yaga's black gown brushed across Sabrina's hand and made her fingers feel as if she had plunged them into a pot of boiling water.

Sabrina closed the door and followed the witch into the living room. Baba Yaga's arrival caused a few of the guests to shuffle uncomfortably. A few even cried out, startled by the hateful woman's presence, but Granny Relda welcomed the old crone warmly and reminded everyone that Baba Yaga was wise to a number of magical secrets. After some grumbling, the guests agreed.

So the odd little party began. The guests discussed every option they could think of. They went up and down the stairs, peeking in on Sabrina's dozing parents, suggesting this spell and that potion, recommending a number of spirits and ancient druidic incantations. Granny Relda followed everyone around, jotting down every idea in the spiral-bound notebook she always kept handy. Mr. Seven suggested that if Charming could be found, he might be the key to waking them up, as his kiss had a reputation for breaking sleeping spells. Sabrina was willing to give it a try until Briar mentioned that the touch of Charming's lips might also make Veronica Grimm fall madly in love with him—as it had done with her. Blushing, Snow White and Cinderella both agreed. It was decided that Charming should be a last resort, as it seemed that his remedy was a package deal. And unless the girls wanted him as a new stepfather, they had to look for another solution.

As the day turned into night the suggestions petered out. And then the meeting was over. The green cookies were eaten and the punch bowl was emptied. The guests wished the Grimms luck and flew off into the night (some literally), and soon the family was alone again, with no surefire solution.

Discouraged, Sabrina crept up to bed. Uncle Jake followed her up the steps with Daphne cradled in his arms. The little girl was sound asleep. Her tiara had slipped down around her neck.

"We're not giving up, 'Brina," Uncle Jake whispered as Sabrina crawled into bed.

"I know," Sabrina said, doing her best imitation of a positive attitude.

Her uncle flipped off the light and closed the door. Sabrina lay waiting for her eyes to adjust to the darkness, waiting to see the little model airplanes that her father had made when he was a boy, waiting for the slope of the ceiling to come into view. She closed her eyes tight and fought back a tear. She was so tired of waiting.

• • •

Sabrina wasn't sure what time it was when she was roused from a deep sleep by someone banging on the door downstairs. She looked over at her snoring sister and crawled out of bed.

"I'll get it," she grumbled.

She crossed the room and went down the steps, feeling the cool hardwood floor beneath her feet. With every step the knocking grew louder and more insistent. As Sabrina turned the doorknob it occurred to her that maybe she should let an adult open the door in the middle of the night. But it was too late. She was already face-to-face with Baba Yaga.

"Did you forget your purse or something?" Sabrina asked.

"You are a thief!" the witch said, pointing her withered finger at Sabrina. Suddenly, an unseen force snatched the girl around the neck and yanked her out of the house and off the ground. "Give it back to me, or I'll break your bones like kindling and feast on their marrow."

With the invisible viselike grip choking her, Sabrina couldn't breathe, let alone deny the witch's accusation. Helpless and lightheaded, she dangled above the ground with her legs kicking wildly.

"If you return what you took, I promise to kill you quickly," Baba Yaga added.

"Hag, Sabrina Grimm is under the protection of the Trickster King," a voice shouted. There was a flutter of wings and Puck flew out of the house with sword in hand. He circled the witch while keeping an eye on the bizarre house stomping around in the front yard. "Leave her be, or you will face the wrath of the Blood King of Faerie, the Prince of the Wrong Side of the Tracks, the beacon of hope for all good-for-nothings, slackers, and delinquents. The spiritual leader of—"

Before Puck could finish his boasting, Baba Yaga raised her free hand. An eruption of energy shot out of her palm and slammed into the fairy boy's chest. The impact was so powerful, it sent him flailing across the yard and far into the field on the other side of the street.

Granny, Daphne, Uncle Jake, and Elvis charged outside.

"Put her down, Old Mother," Granny Relda demanded, though she was rather unintimidating in curlers and fuzzy slippers.

"Your nestling has stolen from me, Relda," Baba Yaga bellowed.

"Put her down, witch," Uncle Jake said. "You're not the only one around here who can wield magic."

Baba Yaga sneered. "Your threats are like the buzzing of a mosquito. Stand still and I'll swat you."

Suddenly, something huge, brown, and furry raced past Sabrina. It slammed into Baba Yaga and the witch crashed to the ground. The assault seemed to break the witch's concentration, and the suffocating grip on Sabrina's throat vanished. She fell to the porch and clutched her neck, forcing air into her burning lungs. Tears filled her eyes, making the world a blur, but she knew what had attacked the witch. Mr. Canis was out of his room, and he was angry.

"I'm standing still. Why don't you swat me?" Canis said as he hovered over the old hag.

Baba Yaga shrieked in rage. She raised her hands and a ball of crackling energy appeared in her palm. Mr. Canis flew backward, smacking roughly against the house, and let out a painful groan. The impact was so violent, Sabrina was sure even Mr. Canis couldn't walk away from it. But with animal-like speed and reflexes, he leaped forward, snatched Baba Yaga off the ground in one of his huge hands, and tossed her at her own house. The crash was devastating. She smashed through the front wall of her shack, leaving a gaping hole between the two filthy windows. The shutters fluttered like eyelids trying to remove a troublesome speck of dust.

Uncle Jake helped Sabrina to her feet. "What did you do that's got her so mad?" he asked.

Sabrina choked. "She thinks I stole something from her."

Just then, Baba Yaga appeared in one of her windows. "She has been touched!" she screamed, pointing directly at Sabrina.

"You're mucho-crazy-o!" Daphne cried as she struggled to hold Elvis back from attacking the witch. "Worse, you're mean. My sister didn't steal anything from you. Leave her alone or things are going to get ugly." The little girl stepped into her attack stance and made her "warrior face"—a slightly comical expression she believed people found intimidating. Luckily, Granny Relda was nearby to grab Daphne and Elvis and pull them into the house.

"Give me my possession or I'll destroy this house and everyone in it," Baba Yaga screamed.

"We have no idea what you are talking about," Granny insisted.

"The Wand of Merlin!" the witch said. "Your nestling has stolen it."

"I didn't take anything from her!" Sabrina cried. "I wouldn't come near her stinking house for a million bucks!"

"Liar! Thief!" Baba Yaga shrieked.

"I believe Sabrina," Granny cried. "She has not been out to your home. Someone else must have taken it. If you want our help getting your wand back, all you have to do is ask, but you're not to come here and threaten my family. I don't care who you are."

Baba Yaga disappeared from her window. A moment later, the front door of her house flew open and she scurried into the Grimms' yard, pointing her gnarled, wart-covered finger at Sabrina. "She—"

"I have never lied to you, Old Mother," Granny interrupted.

Baba Yaga stopped in her tracks. She eyed Granny Relda skeptically, then looked over at Mr. Canis. "You will find the wand?"

Granny nodded. "We'll come out to see you in the morning and then we'll get to the bottom of this."

"Fine!"

"Fine."

The witch turned and hobbled back into her house. A moment later it rose up on its haunches, turned, and lumbered back across the street. It disappeared into the woods, leaving a trail of black chimney smoke in its wake.

Moments later, Puck streaked back into the yard and landed with his sword clenched tightly in his hand. "Where did she go?"

"She's gone," Sabrina said.

"Coward! Of course she ran off," Puck crowed. "She attacked me when I wasn't ready and then ran back to her woods! Miserable sissy!"

"Well, you can settle your dispute with her tomorrow. We're going for a visit," Granny said.

Sabrina turned to her grandmother. "If you think I'm going to that lunatic's house, you're as crazy as she is."

• • •

"This is crazy!" Sabrina shouted as she squished through the mud with her grandmother, Daphne, and Puck. A fresh rain had soaked the woods, turning the forest floor into a swamp. Puck followed Sabrina with his sword in his hand. He muttered to himself about what he planned to do to Baba Yaga when he confronted her, while occasionally remembering to insult Sabrina.

"I hear she eats people, Grimm," he said. "I bet she turns you all into jerky!"

"I don't want to be jerky," Daphne cried.

"No one is going to get turned into jerky," Granny said. "This is going to be nice and pleasant."

"That's what people always say before they become jerky," Puck said. "Don't worry, folks. I've got a score to settle with the witch. She'll regret the day she laid a hand on the Trickster King."

Puck's boasting made Sabrina nervous. Baba Yaga had a two-thousand-year-old reputation for black magic and an even blacker mood. The family journals were filled with rumors of her cannibalism and murders. The last time Sabrina visited her creepy house, Sabrina had had to hop for her life when Baba Yaga turned her into a frog and tried to eat her. The last thing they needed was for Puck to start a fight with the old crone.

They walked until they came upon a part of the forest where the thin, dead trees were close together, their limbs intertwined, as if they were holding one another at the moment of their deaths. Though there was nothing to block the sunshine, the area was dark and gray. Not a blade of grass sprang from the ground. Sabrina realized that the natural sounds of the forest were also gone: the scurrying of animals, the wind in the branches, the crackling of earth beneath their feet—all silenced.

They continued on and soon found themselves on a path of bleached stones. Sabrina had followed it once before and knew where it led—straight to the man-eating witch. She also knew that the stones of the path were not what they seemed. It wasn't long before Puck noticed they were peculiar as well.

"These are human skulls!" he cried, digging one out of the ground and holding it up to the group.

"Don't be frightened, Puck," Granny said.

"Frightened? This is the coolest thing I've ever seen!" the

boy said. He moved the skull's jaw up and down like a spooky puppet and then stuck it next to Daphne's face. "Hey, little girl, how about a smooch?"

Daphne shrieked and hid behind her sister. Granny Relda scolded Puck and demanded he return the skull to the path.

"What happened to your claims of revenge, Trickster King?" Sabrina asked the fairy. "All of a sudden Baba Yaga is like a movie star to you."

"Just because I'm going to unleash hellfire on her doesn't mean I can't appreciate her style," Puck said.

"Granny, what happened to her bodyguards?" Daphne asked as she peered ahead. The notoriously deadly Bright Sun, Black Night, and Red Star—each a bizarre hybrid of an animal and a man—usually guarded the old witch, but they were nowhere in sight.

"Don't worry about them," Puck said. "They won't be showing their ugly faces around here. They know better than to cross paths with me." The boy's voice cracked at the end of the sentence. Puck looked around as if someone else had made the noise. He said the word "me" again with the same result.

"Sounds like you might be coming down with a cold," Granny said.

"Everafters do not get colds!" Puck argued.

"Nonetheless I think I'll make you some chicken soup when we get home."

The group continued down the path and soon Baba Yaga's hut came into view. A fence made from ancient human leg and arm bones surrounded it. Granny Relda pushed open the fence and led the family into the yard. Sabrina eyed her grandmother with awe and envy. The old woman was fearless. She strolled to the front door as if she were visiting an old friend. Sabrina wondered if she would ever feel that courageous.

Granny knocked, and a moment later the door flew open.

"*The Young and the Restless* is on," Baba Yaga seethed. She was holding a bowl of cereal in her hand and eating it with a spoon.

Granny shuffled her feet. "I'm sorry. We thought you'd want us to get started as soon as possible."

The witch frowned but waved everyone into the house. The inside was as disturbing as the outside. In a corner, dusty burlap bags leaked green ooze onto the floor. Along the wall stood stacks of crates, one of which seemed to have something inside struggling to break free. The brick fireplace was lit, and the flames formed the desperate faces of people who seemed to be begging for help. Sabrina shuddered to imagine herself trapped with those poor souls, suffering for eternity in Baba Yaga's home. Still, the most unsettling feeling wasn't the filth and despair that seemed to permeate the air, it was the odd sensation running up and down Sabrina's spine. At first she thought it was just nerves, but she soon realized that what she felt was more like hunger—a nervous, unnatural craving. Every drop of blood, bit of muscle fiber, and strand of hair in her being was awake and starving. She glanced around at the wands, spell books, and magical rings the witch left lying about. Baba Yaga didn't deserve these things. Look how she mistreated them!

"Are you going to be OK?" Daphne asked. She squeezed Sabrina's arm.

Sabrina took a deep breath and nodded. "Let's get out of here as soon as we can."

"Where are your guardians, Old Mother?" Granny Relda asked the witch.

"They failed me," the witch snapped.

"That's not what I asked."

The witch screamed in rage. "Don't question me! I created them for a purpose. They were to guard my possessions. They failed. You needn't know more."

Sabrina could easily read between the lines. Baba Yaga's guardians were dead. Their bones were probably part of the fence outside.

Puck, on the other hand, was completely oblivious to the conversation. He was busy snooping around the room, opening cabinets and peeking into drawers as if he owned the place. "This book looks like it's made out of human skin!" he exclaimed when he picked up a discarded tome off the floor. The cover looked like leather, but had hair growing out of it.

"It is!" Baba Yaga cackled.

Puck looked like he wanted to hug the old hag. "This place is like my Disneyland."

"Uh, hello?" Sabrina said. "What happened to the hellfire?"

Puck scowled and put the book back on the floor.

"Old Mother, tell us what you know about your missing wand," Granny said as she took out her notebook and pen.

"It was here one moment and gone the next," the witch said, flashing Sabrina an accusing look.

"Can you show us where you kept it?" Granny said.

The crone hobbled into the next room. The floor was covered in dust and what looked like human teeth. There was an overstuffed reclining chair in the center of the room, across from a television on a rickety stand against the wall. The jawbone of a ferocious-looking animal rested on top of the TV with an old wire hanger wrapped in tinfoil sticking out of it, making a very disturbing antenna.

"I kept the wand in here," the witch said as she gestured around the room.

"OK, girls. Here's where we get to put your training into action," Granny Relda said. "Have a look around, and remember, keep an eye out for things that are out of place."

In the last two months Granny Relda had been teaching Sabrina and Daphne to see—or rather, to observe—things. She believed good detectives had to use all of their senses to get a true picture of a crime scene. Her method included sniffing for odd scents, listening for unusual sounds, and peeking into dark corners. Sabrina had her own method, though. She believed the best way to find a criminal was to think like one. All she had to do was think about what she might have done if she were trying to get away with something. When she combined her approach with her grandmother's, she discovered that she could spot things that others missed.

She scanned the room, wondering what her grandmother might mean by "out of place." Ancient wallpaper was peeling from the walls—nothing odd there. The old woman wasn't exactly Martha Stewart. The floor had an enormous stain Sabrina hoped wasn't blood. In the far corner was a table covered in vials and little glass jars filled with greenish liquid. All manner of disgusting objects floated inside them.

"Sabrina?" Daphne said. "What do you see?"

Sabrina studied the table but saw nothing unusual, if you

considered a pile of dead chameleons normal. Still, Granny had taught her to be thorough, so she took a peek under the table. There she spotted a small hole in the baseboard. Daphne joined her and pointed out that there were little greasy paw tracks in the dust around the hole. The witch had mice.

"When did you notice the wand was missing?" Granny asked.

"Late last night," the witch said.

"Was anything else taken?"

"No. Do you know who did it yet?"

"We just got here," Granny said.

The witch scowled. "Tomorrow I will take matters into my own hands, Relda Grimm."

"Old Mother, please," Granny pleaded. "You have to give us some time."

"You heard me. Tomorrow!"

3

When the family returned home, Granny sent the children to wash up while she prepared one of her signature dishes—corn flakes in avocado sauce. The old woman was under the impression that the odd recipes she had collected on her adventures around the world were enjoyed by her whole family, but the old woman was very, very wrong. Sabrina couldn't stand her grandmother's cooking. Day after day she had suffered through tulip root soup, Chinese beetle bread, crocodile steaks, creamed bacon with butterscotch nuggets, horseradish-flavored oatmeal, and Limburger pancakes. She might have been able to change the menu if she wasn't surrounded by people who would eat anything. Daphne scarfed down whatever was put in front of her, even dishes that Elvis would turn up his huge snout at, and Elvis wasn't exactly a *New York Times* food critic.

Puck rarely looked at the food he shoved in his mouth, and that afternoon was no different. He kept Granny rushing back to the kitchen to refill his plate. He even tried to steal a couple of rolls from Daphne, but the little girl used her fork to defend them.

"Puck! What is wrong with you?" Granny asked, exhausted.

"I'm starving!" the boy fairy said as he shoved a celery stalk into his mouth. "I could eat a horse and that's not a joke. I should know. I've eaten a horse!"

Daphne let out a little whimper. She had a fondness for ponies.

"Arthenus the World-Smasher bet me I couldn't do it," Puck said between bites. "That rat still owes me a million dollars. He tried to welch when I wouldn't eat the saddle. The saddle is not technically part of the horse, is it?"

Everyone stared at the boy.

"Well, it's not, right?"

Mr. Canis entered the room and took a seat. Squeezing into his chair was getting harder and harder for him. Soon, Sabrina suspected, he wouldn't be able to join them for dinner at all.

"Mr. Canis, our friend Puck has some odd symptoms. Earlier he had a crackling throat and now he can't seem to get enough to eat," Granny said with an odd smile.

Mr. Canis examined Puck closely, then took a deep sniff in Puck's direction. "Interesting."

Puck sat up and turned his head from the old woman to the old man. "What? What's wrong?"

Granny Relda smiled and shook her head. "You'll see."

Puck scowled and turned to Sabrina. He stuck out his tongue, exposing a mouthful of half-chewed food, then laughed when she turned green.

Just then, there was a knock at the door. Sabrina, who had lost her appetite once again, handed the boy her plate and got up from the table. "I'll get it."

She crossed the room and opened the door. Standing on the porch was Morgan le Fay. She looked distraught.

"I need your help," she said. "I've been robbed."

Sabrina sighed. "I think I'm seeing the beginnings of a pattern."

• • •

Everafters unnerved Sabrina. She didn't like talking animals or inanimate objects running around. Trolls gave her the willies, the memory of her encounter with Rumpelstiltskin still haunted her, but witches were the spookiest of them all. Most of the ones she had met were covered in warts and misplaced puffs of hair. They smelled funny and laughed at things that were disturbing. Even the seemingly normal-looking Glinda, who was actually quite pretty, had an odd way of talking—a sort of singsong that grated on Sabrina's nerves. All in all, she could do without witches.

Morgan le Fay, on the other hand, was a beautiful, curvy woman with jet-black hair and big bright eyes. She was funny, smart, and a little sarcastic, which, as a New Yorker, Sabrina held in the highest regard. She also had a seductive charm that made men of all ages crazy. Uncle Jake nearly knocked over the dining room table when Granny asked him if he'd like to drive them to Morgan's house.

The enchantress lived in an apartment not far from the Metro-North train station. Her place was nothing fancy. The pavement leading to the front door was crumbling, the yard was filled with mud and crabgrass, and there were several rusty bikes lying in a neglected shrub out front. Parked by the curb was a van with a giant mouse stepping onto a mousetrap on top. The words RODENT WRANGLERS were painted on the van's doors.

The family followed Morgan as she sashayed to her front door. Waiting there were half a dozen men who quickly removed their hats, straightened their hair, and sucked in their potbellies when they spotted her.

"Morgan," one of the men said. "I fixed that leaky sink."

"Oh, Steven, you're a doll," Morgan said as she reached up and kissed the man on the cheek. "I only called about it yesterday."

"Morgan, I've gone to the hardware store and picked up all the paint for the living room," another man said proudly, as if he had just won a gold medal in the Olympics.

"Morgan, I'll be here bright and early tomorrow to change your oil," another man said.

"Morgan, I put in a new hot water tank for you."

"Morgan, I fixed that crooked mirror in your bathroom."

"Morgan, I spackled that hole in the kitchen ceiling."

"Oh, boys, you really must let me pay you something for all the hard work you're doing," she purred.

"Absolutely not!" the men cried, then turned and shot one another angry, jealous looks.

"Boys, I'm so happy you came by, but I have some guests right now," the beautiful witch said. The men looked as if they had waited in line all day to ride the carousel only to hear the fair was closing for the night. They threw out a few halfhearted "of courses" and promised to return at a time that was more convenient for Morgan. She thanked them all and gave each a hug. The men strutted to the parking lot as if they'd just won the lottery. Moments later, they were arguing. A second after that, they were all in one big fistfight.

"Boys will be boys," Morgan said with an embarrassed smile. She unlocked her apartment door and led the group inside, where Sabrina's ears were assaulted by a terrific racket of rockets, machine guns, and helicopters. She could actually feel the floor rumbling beneath her shoes from the volume. She wondered if she hadn't just stepped onto a battlefield until she noticed a very pale and pudgy young man playing the most violent video game she had ever seen. The man looked to be in his late twenties, though his three-day beard, paunchy belly, and tired eyes made him seem much older. He wore a ratty T-shirt that read ONE RING TO RULE THEM ALL, and he was surrounded by delivery pizza boxes and hamburger wrappers. If he noticed that anyone had entered the room, he made no sign of it.

"Mordred!" Morgan said sharply. "We have company."

"I see them," he said without turning his head.

"Well, turn off your game and say hello!"

"Mom! I'm about to beat the level-fifteen boss! Do you have any idea how many experience points I can get?"

"Fine, if you don't want to socialize and act like an adult, then go to your room and clean it up. I have to vacuum in there, and you've got your dolls all over the place."

Mordred looked over at his mother with a murderous rage in his face. His pupils vanished and his eyes turned pure white and radiated energy.

"THEY'RE NOT DOLLS. THEY'RE ACTION FIGURES!"

He leaped up from the couch and turned off his game. "The exterminator is in the bathroom," he snapped as he marched into a room and slammed the door behind him.

"I'm sorry," Morgan said. "Mordred is a bit—"

"Geeky?" Uncle Jake interrupted.

"Nerdy?" Sabrina offered.

"Mucho lame-o?" Daphne added.

"I was going to say aimless," the witch replied. "I know he's a bit old to be living at home with his mom, but he's had a difficult time holding a job. He's worked at Wendy's, Taco Bell, and Burger King, but it always ends the same way—he challenges his manager to combat, takes over the restaurant, and enslaves his coworkers. Then it's back to video games."

"We'd like to get right down to business, if possible," Granny said without batting an eyelash. "You told us you have been robbed. What was taken?"

"The Wonder Clock," Morgan le Fay answered as she walked around the room picking up empty french-fry boxes.

"No way!" Uncle Jake exclaimed.

"Uh, what's the Wonder Clock?" Sabrina asked. Her father had kept her and Daphne away from fairy-tale stories when they were little, trying to protect them. Unfortunately it put the Grimm sisters at a disadvantage in Ferryport Landing. It seemed as if they hardly knew anything about fairy tales. Lately the girls had made a serious effort to read the original tales as part of their training, but Sabrina hadn't come across the Wonder Clock.

"Howard Pyle wrote about it, *liebling*. The story goes that it was found in the attic of Father Time," Granny explained, then turned her attention back to Morgan. "I was under the impression the Wonder Clock was a myth."

"So was I!" Uncle Jake said. He prided himself on being able to track down magical items, and he always had quite a number of them on his person. His jacket was sewn with extra pockets where he kept enchanted rings, wands, and potions.

"Nope. It's real and it works," Morgan replied.

"Works?" Granny asked. "In what way? Pyle wrote that its only function was to tell stories when the clock struck the hour."

Morgan le Fay shuffled her feet uncomfortably. "Well . . . it does something else."

Uncle Jake grinned eagerly. "What?"

"It's kind of a time machine."

Sabrina laughed. She never knew Morgan had such a great sense of humor.

"No, really," Morgan said. "It lets a person go twelve hours into the past."

"What good is that?" Daphne wondered.

"It comes in very handy when you accidentally say yes to two dates on the same night," the beautiful witch said.

"Morgan, how long has the clock been missing?" Granny asked.

"I'm not sure," the witch replied. "I came home from your party and went straight to bed. It was on the kitchen table when I turned off the lights. This morning it was gone."

"And you didn't hear anything?" Granny asked.

"Nothing. The front door was wide open when I woke up, but I know I locked it."

"What about Mordred?" Uncle Jake asked. "Could he have taken it?"

"No," Morgan said. "He's very honest. He says he has no idea what happened to the clock and I believe him."

Just then, a fat orange creature no more than a foot tall stepped out of the bathroom. It was wearing green camouflage pants, a green shirt, an army helmet, dog tags, and heavy boots. At first glance, it looked like a dressed up pet, but Sabrina realized it was much more. Walking erect on its hind legs, it seemed just as startled to see Sabrina as she was to see it. It shouted "Incoming!" and dove behind the couch.

"Boots, it's OK," Morgan le Fay said, trying to calm the cat down. "It's Relda Grimm and her family."

The cat peeked its head from around the couch. He looked nervous and his whiskers were frantically twitching. "You scared the bejesus out of me," Boots said in a thick New Jersey accent. "I coulda had a nervous breakdown. You gotta warn a guy. I'm a veteran. I've seen terrible things. Makes a guy jumpy."

"So, did you find anything?" Morgan asked.

"Well, Ms. le Fay, I've got good news and bad news," Boots said. "I'll start with the bad news. You have mice."

"Ugh," Morgan groaned. She crossed the room to her handbag and showed it to the cat. "I knew it! One of them chewed through my purse." She reached into the bag and poked a finger into a small hole near the bottom. "What's the good news?"

"There is no good news. I just thought it might help to have some hope. My advice is to pack your things, burn this place to the ground, and start somewhere new."

"You want her to abandon her home because she has a mouse?" Sabrina said incredulously.

"It's the only chance you have. There is nothing you can do to stop vermin. They just keep coming and coming and coming, haunting your dreams, eating your cereal! Oh, the horror . . ." The cat gazed vacantly as if trapped inside a troubling memory.

"What's 'vermin' mean?" Daphne whispered.

"Vermin are pests like rats, mice, and cockroaches," Sabrina explained.

Daphne's face contorted with disgust. "Gross!"

"I'm going to have to check the basement to make sure you

don't have a nest," Boots said, though Sabrina could see he was visibly trembling.

Sabrina tugged on her grandmother's sleeve. "We saw a mouse hole at Baba Yaga's house," she reminded her.

Granny winked at Sabrina and then turned to Boots. "A mouse, you say? Mind if we take a look?"

"What about my missing clock?" Morgan asked.

"It's possible that it's connected," Granny replied.

Boots eyed the family suspiciously. "I have to tell you, Relda. This could get dangerous. We might not all make it back alive."

"Looking for mice?" Sabrina asked.

"They're vile, unpredictable creatures. They're all teeth, fur, and claws."

"We'll try to be careful," Granny Relda said.

"Don't say I didn't warn you," Boots cried.

"If you find anything, please let me know," Morgan said to Uncle Jake, running her hand down his arm. "Oh, strong."

"Yeah, I lift weights from time to time," he bragged.

Granny grabbed her son by the other arm and pulled him outside. "You can be so embarrassing sometimes, Jacob."

Boots led the family around the building and down a flight of steps to the basement. When he unlocked the door, he turned to the family and raised a finger to his mouth. "Shhh! They've got great hearing."

The basement was damp and cluttered. There were stacks of moldy cardboard boxes, a collection of poorly laced tennis rackets, an artificial Christmas tree still covered in tinsel, and an old coffee table with a wobbly leg. Boots weaved his way through the room, staring up at the cobweb-strewn rafters. He explained that he needed to be directly under Morgan le Fay's apartment. Once he found the spot, he took a flashlight off of his tool belt and shined it along the walls and ceiling.

"What are you looking for?" Daphne whispered, peering into the shadows.

"A nest," Boots purred. "Or a hole in the ceiling. They could be chewing their way into Morgan's apartment."

"A mouse can chew through a floorboard?" Sabrina asked. It seemed impossible that a tiny creature could do that kind of damage.

Boots shook his head. "Only a fool would underestimate a mouse's capabilities. They can squeeze through a hole a quarter of their size. They can chew through concrete and jump up to twelve inches. Plus, they're ravenous. They've got to eat fifteen to twenty times a day, so they're highly motivated. When you combine that with how many babies they make in a year—

upwards of a hundred—you can see we are under assault. They're coming for us, kid. They're going to take over the world. It's not a matter of if . . . it's a matter of when."

Just then, Daphne brushed against a cardboard box, knocking it to the ground. There was a heavy thump and clang, but Boots acted as if someone had just set off an explosion. He leaped behind a chair and shouted for everyone to get down.

"We're under attack!" he shouted.

Granny helped him back to his feet and assured him the invasion had not yet begun. When he had calmed himself, he went back to his search.

"There's no holes down here and no tracks upstairs. I suspect it was only one mouse. Morgan probably carried it in from outside. They can leap onto a coat and cling to it for days. Mice are sneaky. In fact, their name comes from a Sanskrit word for thief."

"Could it be something other than a mouse?" Uncle Jake asked.

"Like what?"

"Oh, I don't know—a little person, perhaps a Lilliputian?"

"Sorry, Jake, that's not my specialty, but anything's possible."

Granny reached into her handbag and found a pen and a small scrap of paper. "Would you call us if there are any other unexplained situations like this one?"

Boots nodded. "You on some big case, Relda?"

Granny smiled. "We are Grimms. This is what we do."

• • •

"I can't believe the effect that woman had on me," Uncle Jake said as they drove through town. "I think she's got some kind of magic over men."

"I half expected you to offer to scrub her floors," Granny grumbled.

Uncle Jake laughed. "Don't worry, Mom. I'm not going to bring a witch into the family. I've got my eye on a princess."

"You should have had your eye on finding clues," Granny scolded him. She turned in her seat and looked at the girls. "Well?"

Sabrina and Daphne gaped at her.

"What are you asking *us* for?" Sabrina sputtered.

"Because you two are detectives. This is your case. What have you detected so far?" the old woman asked.

Daphne shrugged, causing Sabrina to grimace. She was hoping her little sister had noticed something she hadn't.

"C'mon, girls," Granny begged. "What do these two robberies have in common?"

"Stolen magical items," Daphne said.

"Correct!"

"Um, both were robbed by someone that the victims never saw?" Sabrina added.

"Excellent!"

"Both of the people who were robbed were witches," Daphne added.

"And both have a mouse problem," Sabrina said.

"So you have been paying attention," Granny said with a grin.

"You think mice broke into their homes and stole their stuff?" Sabrina asked with a snort. "You sound as crazy as that cat!"

"Uh, hello? We're in Ferryport Landing," Uncle Jake said. "It's more than possible."

"The Three Blind Mice live in the town, as well as the Mouse King of Oz and his people," Granny said. "In fact, there are quite a number of mice living in this town, but I have what detectives call 'a hunch.'"

"You think the criminal is something other than a mouse?" Uncle Jake asked.

"Possibly. You mentioned Lilliputians back at Morgan's house. We did have to put an end to one of their crime sprees a while back."

"But all the Lilliputians are in the town jail," Daphne said.

"Then I suppose it's time to pay them a visit," the old woman replied.

Sabrina and Daphne exchanged a look.

"The new sheriff is not exactly one of your fans," Uncle Jake said. "Do you really think he'll be cooperative?"

"Perhaps not." Granny Relda sighed. "But it can't hurt to ask."

"Actually, I think it could hurt a lot," Sabrina said. Before Sheriff Nottingham was elected, the legendary villain of the Robin Hood story swore that when he became sheriff, he'd devote every waking hour to locking the Grimm family behind bars.

Uncle Jake drove the family to the police station and parked the car on the street. The first thing Sabrina noticed was that the bicycle store next door had closed. A big sign in the window said GOING OUT OF BUSINESS.

"I guess I can cross that off the list," Sabrina said. One of her birthday wishes was for a bicycle.

"It appears times are tough all over," Granny Relda said as she pointed across the street. An antiques store and a florist were also boarded up, each with signs hanging in the window that read SORRY, WE'RE CLOSED.

Entering the police station felt like climbing into the mouth of a lion. The new sheriff was cold, calculating, and carried a dagger with him wherever he went. Luckily, he was not in the lobby when the family stepped inside. Christmas decorations hung from the walls and a needle-less pine was rotting in the corner with a few multicolored bulbs still clinging to its decaying limbs. These were decorations Sheriff Hamstead and his deputies, Swineheart and Boarman, had set up back in December. It was just one example of the office's neglect. An inch of dust covered most surfaces, leaning towers of files spilled their contents onto the filthy floor, and many of the desk chairs were broken and lying on the ground. There was no one at the front counter or anywhere else. The only new addition to the station was a full-length mirror leaning against a wall.

"Hello!" Granny called out.

"Maybe he's gone," Sabrina said hopefully. "We should come back."

Before anyone could take her advice, a door at the far end of the room opened and Sheriff Nottingham entered. He was a tall, angry man with long black hair that fell past his shoulders. He had a jagged scar that ran from the bottom of one of his dark eyes to the corner of his lips. A goatee framed his wicked mouth.

"What do you want?" he growled as he limped over to the desk. Sabrina remembered that the injury was the result of one of Robin Hood's well-aimed arrows.

Granny forced a smile onto her face. "Sheriff, we haven't had the opportunity to talk since you were elected. I thought it best if we came down and said hello. I'm sure you're aware of my family's history in Ferryport Landing. I know the previous administration found our unique talents very helpful. I wanted to extend my hand with the hope we'll be able to work together for the good of the town."

"Extend your hand, woman, and you'll find me lopping it off with a sword," Nottingham seethed.

Uncle Jake stepped forward. "You talk like that to my mother again, pal, and you and I are going to have a big problem."

The sheriff pulled his coat aside to reveal his shiny dagger. "Our problems have yet to begin."

Uncle Jake pulled his jacket aside to reveal hundreds of blinking rings, wands, and jewels. "If you're feeling froggy, Sheriff—take a leap."

The two men stared at each other tensely.

"Why are you here?" Nottingham demanded.

"We're investigating a series of robberies—"

Nottingham quickly cut her off. "I haven't received any reports about robberies."

"I suppose you will once the citizens get to know you," Granny said. "But these are close friends, and we're just helping out. Our investigation has led us here. We'd appreciate it if we could speak to the Lilliputians."

Nottingham laughed. "I'm afraid I couldn't do that even if I wanted to. I released all the Everafter prisoners when I became sheriff."

"You did *what*?" Granny cried. "Some of those people were dangerous."

"Says you. This town is no longer your playground, Mrs. Grimm," Nottingham barked. "You and your meddling family have had your fun, and now it is over. Luckily, you won't be around much longer."

"What's that supposed to mean?" Uncle Jake asked, already reaching into his pockets for a weapon.

"I'm talking about the tax."

"The tax?" Sabrina said.

"The property tax," Nottingham said with a smile. "What? Didn't you get the letter?"

"What letter?" Granny said.

Nottingham reached into a desk and pulled out a typed form. He threw it at Sabrina, who scanned it quickly and then read the first paragraph aloud. "'Property Tax Assessment. The town of Ferryport Landing has recently reassessed the value of your property, resulting in additional tax. Your estimated obligation is one hundred and fifty thousand dollars.'"

"One hundred and fifty thousand dollars!" Granny groaned.

"Yes, public services aren't free. There are schools and roads to maintain, and of course the Police Department. Everyone is going to have to pay their fair share."

"Even you?" Uncle Jake said.

"Me?" Nottingham laughed. "I'm exempt. I'm an Everafter."

"You're only taxing the humans?" Granny Relda asked.

Uncle Jake growled. "You dirty, filthy, rotten—"

"Ferryport Landing is an Everafter settlement," Nottingham said. "Too many outsiders have come in here, stealing our jobs, enjoying our hospitals and schools. But not for much longer. Mayor Heart has decreed, and I wholeheartedly agree, that Ferryport Landing is an Everafter town for Everafters!"

"You've sent this letter to every human in town? What if the people can't pay?" Granny Relda asked.

"Then we'll repossess their property."

"What does 'repossess' mean?" Daphne whispered in Sabrina's ear.

"It means they can take our house and kick us out into the street," Sabrina replied, quickly realizing why the bike shop, florist, and antiques store had closed their doors.

Daphne turned to Nottingham. "Where will we go?"

"That's not the town's concern," Nottingham said, cracking his knuckles. "But don't worry. You have until Friday to pay your bill."

That's only two days away, Sabrina thought.

• • •

Sabrina watched out the window as the car cruised through the little town. She felt as if she were seeing it for the first time. It hadn't been long ago when she had thought Ferryport Landing was boring and old-fashioned, but she had learned to love it. Now it was disappearing right before her eyes. Moving trucks were parked outside of homes as burly men loaded beds, wardrobes, record players, and clothes onto them. Everyone, it appeared, was having a yard sale, hawking their most prized possessions in hopes of paying the tax or having something to start a new life somewhere else. She imagined Nottingham and Mayor Heart driving through the town and rubbing their greedy hands together, cackling at the troubles they had heaped on the human population.

"This is nothing to worry about," Granny Relda said, though her expression didn't match her confident words. She kept reading and rereading the tax letter. "Nothing to worry about at all."

"Granny, do we have a hundred and fifty thousand dollars?" Daphne asked.

The old woman shook herself out of a daze. "I'm sorry, *liebling*. What did you say?"

"Do we have the money to pay the taxes?"

Granny flinched at the question, like she had been stung by a bee. "We'll be fine, girls," she said to them, but Sabrina was already nervous. During her time in the orphanage, and later in dozens of foster homes, she had acquired the ability to recognize a lying adult.

• • •

Later that evening, the girls dressed in their white martial arts robes, called *Gi*s. The uniform consisted of white pants and a robe shirt with a sash of colored cloth used as a belt. Sabrina helped Daphne wrap her brown belt around her waist and then tied her own yellow one. The colors represented levels of expertise; brown was for beginners, yellow was more advanced. Once the girls were ready, they met Puck in the hallway. Dressed in his usual jeans and green hooded sweatshirt, he had a big black scarf wrapped around his waist.

"I think you have to *earn* your black belt," Daphne said.

Puck rolled his eyes. "I'm already the best butt-kicker in this town. They don't even have a color for how good I am."

Sabrina shrugged and unlocked the spare-room door that led to her sleeping parents and Mirror. After kissing her parents on the cheek, Sabrina led the others through the reflection, where they found Mirror sitting in a chair enjoying a glass of brandy and some expensive chocolates.

"Snow's down the hall," he said, pointing. "Have fun!"

The children walked the way Mirror had pointed and soon

found the gorgeous teacher waiting for them near the rooms that held magical hats and "Tooth Fairy Teeth." Snow wore a white robe like the girls', but with a black belt wrapped around her waist. She had her long dark hair tied up in a bun and was barefoot.

"Hello, children," she said, bowing.

"Hello, sensei," Sabrina and Daphne said together as they bowed back to her. Puck, however, was picking his nose.

"Tonight we are going to continue to work on our blocking," Ms. White said.

Puck let out an exasperated groan. "Again! When are we going to learn to punch someone in the face?"

Snow White sighed. "Puck, I told you when you asked to join the girls' training sessions that martial arts are not about attack. They're about defense."

"Well, I'm starting my own martial art then," he said. "It's called Puck-fu and there's only one move you need to learn— the knuckle sandwich."

"Well, I wish you luck with that, but Mrs. Grimm and I feel that the girls should learn to *defend* themselves against attackers," Ms. White said. "Now, everyone, let's get into our defensive stance."

Ms. White moved among the group, throwing training punches that allowed the children to block her attacks with ease. As the night rolled on, the attacks became more forceful. They worked on closehanded and openhanded blocks, how to step aside to avoid a punch, and how to use their own wrists to stop an assault. Ms. White was a patient teacher, though Sabrina could tell she was a bit preoccupied. She knew that Charming's disappearance was weighing heavy on Ms. White's heart. Sabrina wanted to reach out to her, but what could she say? She certainly felt sympathy for Snow's worries and broken heart, but Charming was a jerk. He had never done anything that wasn't in his own interest. He'd only ever helped the Grimms to impress Ms. White or to advance his own career. Sabrina wondered what the teacher even saw in the pompous blowhard. Sure, he was breathtakingly handsome, but once he opened his mouth he turned into a first-class lout. Still, she felt she should say something.

"He'll turn up," she said softly.

Ms. White looked as if she were fighting back tears. "I hope so," she whispered, then told the children she would see them in a couple of days for their next class. The girls walked with her out of the Hall of Wonders, downstairs, and then outside, waving when her car pulled out of the driveway.

Sabrina closed the door and went to the dining room where Puck was wolfing down some kind of soup. There was a note on the table from Granny explaining that she had gone to bed early, that Mr. Canis was in his room, and that Uncle Jake had gone out for the night. She advised the children to have as much soup as they wanted and then to get to work researching tiny people and any small animals that might be capable of stealing magical items. Sabrina was dumbfounded. After their run-in with Nottingham and the news of the tax assessment she had completely forgotten they were even involved in a mystery.

"She must be worried," Daphne said as she peered into the pot. "There's nothing purple in the food."

Sabrina poured some soup into a bowl for her sister and then did the same for herself. Then they sat with Puck, who, after several threats, surrendered a few of the rolls he had been hoarding.

"You better be nice to me, piggy," Puck said with a mouthful of soup. "When you two are homeless, you're going to want to live with me in the forest and I'm not going to let just anyone live in *my* forest!"

"Are we really going to be homeless?" Daphne asked.

"No!" Sabrina said.

"Don't lie to her," Puck chimed in. "Things are bleak, marshmallow. If I were you, I'd eat as much of this soup as you can. It might be the last meal you get for a long time. Hoboes have to eat out of garbage cans and beg for crusts of bread in the street."

"I don't want to be a hobo," Daphne said, then turned to her sister. "What's a hobo?"

Sabrina ignored the question and got up from the table.

"Give me that roll, and I'll find you a nice warm refrigerator box to sleep in," Puck said.

"Daphne, don't listen to him," Sabrina said.

Daphne glanced at her sister but surrendered her roll to the boy.

"We need to get to work," Sabrina said with a sigh.

"Well, that's my cue," Puck said as he pushed back from the table. He had once claimed he was allergic to books and that people who tried to improve their minds were just admitting stupidity. He flew off to his room and left the girls alone.

Sabrina went to the bookshelves to begin her search for anything on little thieves. She found some books by Tiny Tim, Thumbelina, and one titled *Life Is Futile*, by Itsy Bitsy Spider. She scooped them all up, set them on the table, then went back to scan the collection of family journals. Every Grimm since Wilhelm, the man who brought the Everafters to Ferryport Landing, had documented his or her experiences in the town. Each journal was packed with eyewitness accounts, and they frequently proved very helpful in solving cases.

For hours, Sabrina and Daphne pored over the old books. They read about the Mouse King of Oz, who ruled a million mice; sorted through the various campaigns of an army of tin soldiers; and learned about the history of Lilliput. But they found nothing concrete and soon they came to a dead end. It was very late and they were very tired. Even Elvis was asleep under the table.

"I thought detective work was supposed to be exciting," Sabrina said, closing the book that lay before her.

"I'm excited," Daphne said.

"You're always excited," Sabrina replied, resting her head on the giant oak dining room table they used as a desk. "Granny has probably solved this case already and won't tell us what she knows."

"We're training," Daphne reminded her. "She wants us to figure this out for ourselves."

"She wants to drive us crazy. This town is filled to the brim with talking animals and tiny people, not to mention witches who might be able to shrink themselves. How can we narrow it down?"

"We'll figure it out," Daphne said. "Remember, we're a great team."

Sabrina was tired but she had to smile. "C'mon, Elvis, you've probably got to go out," Sabrina said as she got up from the table.

The big dog nearly knocked Sabrina over as he charged for the front door. Sabrina opened it and Elvis barreled out. "Don't go far," she shouted at the dog, then crossed back through the dining room on her way to the kitchen.

"I'm getting some water," she said to her sister. "Want anything?"

Daphne shook her head. She was half asleep with her head resting on a big book about a village in Oz whose citizens were made of jigsaw-puzzle pieces.

Sabrina went into the kitchen, took a glass from the cupboard, and opened the refrigerator. Inside, there were several containers of leftovers, a package of bologna, and a bowl with a little sign on it that read DANGER! SAUSAGES! KEEP AWAY FROM ELVIS AT ALL COSTS! Sabrina knew the explosive effect they had on the dog. She reached past them for the jug of water her uncle kept in the fridge. She poured some into her glass. Tilting her head back, she took a long refreshing drink and let the cool liquid cascade down her throat. Then she heard Elvis's angry bark.

She peered out of the kitchen window and saw the big dog growling and barking at the edge of the woods. Puck was probably in the backyard preparing another humiliating trap for her, or maybe Elvis was spooked by the odd swirling clouds hovering over the house. Elvis hated thunder and lightning and often hid under the girls' bed during particularly loud storms.

She turned to put the jug back in the refrigerator but spun back around when she heard a loud cry. Sabrina bolted to the window. There in the moonlight she saw her uncle Jake running through the yard. He looked panicked. Suddenly there was a whipping sound, and he crashed to the ground. An arrow was stuck in his back.

4

abrina dropped her glass, and it shattered on the kitchen floor. The crash snapped her out of her shock and she sprang into action. She raced into the dining room, pulled her sister from her chair, and shoved her under the table.

"Stay here!" she ordered, then ran for the front door, shouting for Granny and Mr. Canis. In her bare feet, she raced outside and around the corner into the backyard. She found her uncle lying facedown. Sabrina gently turned him over and he let out a groan.

"Uncle Jake!" she cried, though looking at him closely, she wasn't positive that he was her uncle. There was something wrong with his face. He had a goatee and a large scar on his neck that looked as if a rope had been tied around it. His hair was gray on the sides and his eyes seemed dull. He was clearly in a great deal of pain.

"'Brina?"

"Granny and Mr. Canis are going to help you. They're on their way," Sabrina said through sobs.

"'Brina, you look so young," he said. "You look just like you did when you were twelve."

He's raving from the pain, Sabrina thought to herself. *He needs a doctor right away.* "Someone help us!" she yelled. The storm above was incredibly loud, so she shouted again. She climbed to her feet and turned to the house. "Help!"

Elvis joined her cries with baleful barking, and in no time, Granny and Mr. Canis were rushing out of the house.

"*Liebling*, what is the matter?" Granny begged. She was in her nightgown and slippers and had a green mud mask on her face.

"It's Uncle Jake. He's been hurt," Sabrina cried, turning to the fallen man. But there was no sign of him. Bewildered, Sabrina scanned the edge of the woods. How could he have crawled away so quickly, and without her noticing? She studied the lawn, searching for a trail of blood, but there was nothing.

"But . . . he was lying right here on the ground. I saw him. I saw the arrow! He was dying."

Elvis rushed to the place where Uncle Jake had been lying. He sniffed the ground and whined.

"Child, you are mistaken," Canis said. "I can smell such things. No one has been injured."

"Sabrina, it's late. You must have been having a bad dream," Granny said. "Your Opa Basil used to walk in his sleep too."

"*No!* I saw him. He was right here. We have to look for him!" she cried.

Uncle Jake walked around from the front of the house. He was his normal self. No scar on his neck and no goatee. "What's all the commotion?"

Sabrina suddenly felt woozy. Her eyes filled with little flashes of light and her face grew hot. "You were hurt . . . ," she tried to say, but then everything went black.

• • •

When Sabrina awoke the next morning she felt as if she had been asleep for a hundred years. She was groggy and awkward, and her legs felt like cooked spaghetti as she descended the steps to join her family for breakfast. When she saw that Uncle Jake was working his way through a box of donuts, she began to wonder if her grandmother was right. Maybe the entire incident had just been a vivid nightmare.

"Feeling better?" Granny said, entering the dining room

with a tray of what looked like magenta-colored hash browns. The old woman scooped a spoonful on everyone's plate and a second helping onto Puck's. Elvis hovered under the table, licking Sabrina's feet as if to remind her that he had seen the odd incident as well.

"I'm fine," Sabrina said, though her head felt full of sludge.

"We were worried when you fainted. I fear you may have accidentally touched something at Baba Yaga's house that made you hallucinate," Granny said.

"What does 'hallucinate' mean?" Daphne asked.

"It's when you think you see something that isn't really there," Sabrina said.

"It usually means you've lost your marbles," Puck added.

"We're going to have to be more careful when we go back," their grandmother said as she sat down to eat.

"Go back?" Sabrina exclaimed. "There's no way we're setting foot in that loony-bin again!"

"I can't wait to go back," Puck said. "Baba Yaga is very punk rock."

"Sabrina, of course we have to go back when we find her wand," Granny said, kissing her on the forehead. "Now, hurry up and eat and then get dressed. We've got a another busy day ahead of us."

"Are we back on the case?" Daphne asked in between bites.

Granny nodded. "But first we have to pay our taxes."

• • •

The courthouse was a grand building with a dome and marble columns. It sat just a few doors down from the police station. Outside, a huge crowd of people milled around carrying signs and shouting angrily.

"Looks like a protest," Sabrina said, noticing a sign that had the word TAX painted on it with a big red slash through it.

Mr. Canis pulled the car over to the side of the road to park. "Relda, I don't believe it would be wise for me to walk through that crowd in my current condition."

Granny agreed. "Yes, a seven-foot man with a tail might attract some attention. Stay here. We'll be back in a jiffy."

The Grimms eased their way through the angry mob and up the steps of the building. The people they passed looked desperate. An elderly man grabbed Sabrina by the arm and pleaded, "They can't do this to us. We've got nowhere to go."

Frightened, Sabrina pulled away and caught up with her grandmother and sister. They entered the double doors of the courthouse and immediately spotted an armed guard who gave them directions to the tax assessor's office.

"Is there much of a line?" Granny asked the man.

The guard shook his head. "You're the first people I know of who have the money to pay."

Following his directions, they soon came to a door at the end of a long narrow hallway. TAX ASSESSOR'S OFFICE was stenciled on the door and a little red tag hanging from the doorknob read BE BACK IN 15 MINUTES.

"I guess we have to wait," Granny said.

Fifteen minutes turned into two and a half hours. Eventually they spotted a short, stocky person approaching from the other end of the hallway. As she came closer Sabrina recognized Mayor Heart, the former "Queen of Hearts" from the famous Alice adventures documented by Lewis Carroll. Sabrina thought she looked like a demented beauty pageant contestant. Her face was painted in bold, harsh colors—bloodred lips, dark purple eye shadow, mahogany brown eyebrows, and a black hole of a beauty mark on her left cheek. She was wearing an elaborate crimson gown of silk and lace that had little red hearts sewn into it. She also held an electronic megaphone in one bloated pink hand. The angry mob followed behind her, waving their tax assessment letters in the air furiously. Mayor Heart seemed to be enjoying their frustration and hopelessness, or perhaps she had applied a permanent smile with her obnoxious makeup. Sabrina couldn't be sure.

"People, what's done is done," Mayor Heart said through the entirely too-loud megaphone. Her words blasted the people and echoed off the walls, causing a high-pitched feedback that rang in everyone's ears. "The city needs the funds, and you're going to pay them or you're going to move."

"I'll get a lawyer!" a man threatened.

"Feel free," Heart snapped. "But I have a feeling any lawyer in this town is in the same boat as you. Now, get lost or I'll have the sheriff lock you all up."

"For what?" one man shouted. "It's still legal to protest in this county."

"Then I'll have you locked up for being ugly. Now, scram!"

The people filed out slowly, muttering threats at the mayor until she and the Grimm family were left alone. Heart looked at them and let out a little laugh. She took out a key and unlocked the door to the tax assessor's office, snatching the little note off the door as she stepped inside.

Granny Relda and the girls followed her through the door. They found themselves in a small, windowless office lined with big gray file cabinets. There was a single well-worn counter separating the room into an office area and a waiting area. Heart stepped behind the counter and set a bell down on top of it.

"Good morning, Mayor Heart," Granny said as she stepped up to the counter.

The mayor said nothing. In fact, she opened up a drawer, took out a newspaper, and started reading the day's headlines.

"Hello?" Sabrina said.

Daphne tugged on her grandmother's sleeve and pointed to a sign on the wall. It read RING BELL FOR SERVICE.

Granny looked as if she might leap over the counter and strangle Mayor Heart, but she took a deep breath, reached over, and lightly tapped the bell. The mayor looked up from her paper and flashed the family a forced smile filled with crooked yellow teeth. "Can I help you?"

"Mayor Heart, I didn't realize that you were required to collect taxes personally," Granny said.

"Oh, I'm not," the mayor said with a twisted giggle. "But this job is just too much fun to let someone else do it. I suppose you're here to see if you can talk your way out of your debt too?"

"Not at all," Granny said as she fished in her handbag and took out a stack of money. "I'm here to pay the bill."

The mayor's face turned bright red even through her white pancake makeup. She tried to speak but fell into a coughing fit for several moments before she managed to squeak out, "You what?"

"I said we've come to pay our taxes. This is the correct office?"

The mayor stammered and looked as if she might lapse into another fit. "Yes, it is."

"Very well," the old woman said as she placed the stack of cash in the mayor's hand. "One hundred and fifty thousand dollars."

Ms. Heart reached underneath the counter and snatched her megaphone. She lifted it to her mouth, pushed the button, and bellowed, "NOTTINGHAM!" The feedback rattled Sabrina's ears.

A moment later, the foul sheriff hobbled into the office. "I hear you, woman! If you haven't noticed, I'm a little busy. There's a mob outside, and some fool on Mount Taurus swears he's seen a dinosaur running around up there. Can you believe that? A dinosaur! I put him in a cell for being intoxicated."

"Who cares?" the mayor bellowed into her megaphone. "The Grimms have arrived to pay their taxes."

Nottingham laughed long and hard, but then seemed to realize his boss was not joking. He slammed his fist down on the counter, cursed, and spit on the floor.

"Why, the two of you act as if you're disappointed that we can pay," Granny said, obviously enjoying the change in mood. Sabrina could have sworn she heard sarcasm in her grandmother's voice.

Nottingham snatched the money out of the mayor's hand, flipped through it as if he suspected it were counterfeit, and then slammed it on the table.

"We're going to need a receipt," Granny said sweetly.

Mayor Heart snarled. Then she snatched a book of receipts off a nearby desk, scribbled onto one of them, and ripped it out of the book.

"This isn't over," Heart said, dangling the receipt out of the reach of Granny Relda.

"Oh, we never doubted that for a second," the old woman replied, grabbing the receipt. She placed it safely into her handbag, took the girls by the hand, and escorted them out of the office.

"Have a nice day," Daphne said just before they closed the door.

Sabrina heard the mayor and the sheriff scream in frustration as the family walked back down the hallway. They stepped outside, and for a moment the three Grimms gazed down at the throngs of desperate citizens.

"These poor people," Granny Relda said. "If we had enough I'd give them all the money they need."

"There's not enough money in the world," Sabrina replied. "Mayor Heart wants them out of Ferryport Landing. Anyway, we should be worried about us. What are we going to do if we're the last human family left in the town?"

"I don't know, *liebling*," the old woman said as they stepped into the street. "But for now we should get back to our mystery. Who knows when Baba Yaga is going to lose her patience."

Suddenly, Sheriff Nottingham rushed through the crowd, waving a paper over his head. "Oh, Mrs. Grimm . . ."

"Sheriff, is there a problem?" Granny asked.

"Indeed," Nottingham said. Sabrina couldn't help but stare at the horrible scar that ran down the man's face. She wondered if that was what made him so ugly or if he had been grotesque before the knife had done its work. "It appears we've miscalculated the tax on your property."

"Oh, a refund," Granny said, clapping her hands.

"Bah!" the man said with a sick laugh. "The audit on your house failed to calculate the value of the land it is built on. You have nearly three acres of incredibly valuable property. I'm afraid we need to *add* to your tax liability."

"How much more?" Sabrina said suspiciously.

"Oh, just another three hundred thousand dollars," the sheriff replied.

"That's outrageous!" Granny Relda cried.

"It is, isn't it," Nottingham said as a sinister grin crept across his face.

"And when we pay this, what are you going to tax next? The

air around the house? You're just trying to get rid of us!" Sabrina shouted.

"Well, Mrs. Grimm, your girls are a lot more clever than I was led to believe," the sheriff said. "By the way, the taxes are still due on Friday."

When they got home, Granny Relda was dazed and distant, talking to herself in German. She made some peanut-butter-and-rose-petal sandwiches for the girls and Puck and then asked Uncle Jake and Mr. Canis for a moment of their time. The three adults climbed the steps upstairs for some privacy.

"This is bad," Daphne said.

"Don't worry, marshmallow. You'll get used to the cold," Puck said as he slathered mustard all over his sandwich.

"Granny will come up with an answer," Sabrina said angrily. She flashed the boy a look that said "shut your trap."

Moments later, Uncle Jake returned. "Good news, girls. I'm going to help you with your case. Your grandmother is a little busy with the financials, but it's nothing to worry about."

"Granny said that yesterday when we only owed a hundred and fifty thousand dollars," Daphne reminded him.

"It's all details. Now, where are we on the case?"

"At a dead end," Sabrina reminded him.

"Any suspects?"

"Too many to count," Daphne said.

Uncle Jake scratched his head. "Well, let's put our noggins together for a second. Both the victims had something magical stolen from them. Whoever or whatever stole the objects was pretty small. The victims were both Everafters. What else do they have in common?"

Daphne spoke up. "They're both women."

"They're both very powerful," Sabrina added.

"They were both here the other night," Puck said without looking up from his fourth sandwich. Everyone turned to look at him. Sabrina was shocked that the boy fairy had even noticed.

"That's a good point, Puck," Uncle Jake said. "Both of our victims visited us two nights ago."

"Do you think there might be a connection?" Sabrina asked.

"Could be," Uncle Jake said. "Let's go ask some of the others that came by. Maybe they've got something missing too."

"There were a lot of guests. Who should we see first?" Daphne asked.

Uncle Jake grinned. "Let's go talk to Briar."

Sabrina rolled her eyes.

As they drove through the town, Uncle Jake chattered on about how pretty Briar Rose was, how smart Briar Rose was, how he hoped Briar Rose wasn't mixed up in the mystery. After a while, even Daphne got tired of hearing him sing the princess's praises. Puck threatened to leap from the car several times to end his misery, and Sabrina was considering joining him.

Luckily, Briar's place of business was not far. Ms. Rose owned a quaint little coffee shop three blocks from the courthouse. It bordered the Hudson River, not far from the train station and a tiny marina. Sacred Grounds, as it was called, was a favorite of coffee fanatics. The chalkboard outside promised dozens of different coffees, from espressos to something called a cafe macchiato. It also advertised a variety of muffins, scones, cookies, and donuts. Sabrina had passed the shop many times and noted that it was always jam-packed with customers. Coffee seemed to have the same effect on adults as magic did on her. She remembered her own mother waiting in line for an hour to buy a seven-dollar latte.

Once outside the store Uncle Jake ran his fingers through his hair, blew into his hand to make sure his breath was sweet, and straightened the collar of his shirt.

"How do I look?" he asked the children.

"Why do you care? She's just a girl," Puck said. "Girls are disgusting."

"You won't always feel like that," Uncle Jake said.

"Want to bet?"

"You look mucho handsome-o," Daphne said, straightening the cuff of her uncle's coat.

Uncle Jake winked at the little girl, then led everyone into the shop. It was wall-to-wall with people: chatting, working on laptop computers, and sipping from tall, frothy cups of coffee. There were several little tables scattered about and a bright glass case in the front filled with pastries. There was also a long line of impatient, agitated people.

Sabrina spotted Briar Rose behind the counter. Even with her hair pulled back and an apron tied around her waist, she was a knockout. She worked the cash register, ringing up orders and keeping the line moving as quickly as possible, which wasn't easy. Most of the customers wanted coffees with ridiculously long names and detailed preparation instructions.

"I want a large decaf nonfat soy iced latte with sugar-free hazelnut."

"Give me a triple red-eye espresso, over lactose-free milk with canesugar."

"One extra-large chai tea swirl with a dash of fresh cinnamon."

The family got into the line and slowly worked their way to the counter.

"Jacob," Ms. Rose said sweetly when it was their turn.

"Briar," he replied. "You look amazing."

The princess blushed. "You always say that."

"It's always true."

"Don't distract her," said a little old woman at the end of the line. "I need my caffeine and I need it now!"

"Sorry, Mrs. Finnegan," the princess said. "It'll only take a second."

"C'mon, pal," a man shouted from the middle of the line. "We've been here a long time."

Sabrina cringed. "They're going to kill us all right here in the store."

"Briar, what is the holdup?" Mallobarb asked as she approached from behind the counter, Buzzflower by her side. When the fairy godmothers spotted Uncle Jake, they scowled.

"Only paying customers," Buzzflower said angrily.

"Hello, ladies, we're happy to buy something," Uncle Jake said. "In fact, we haven't had lunch yet. I suppose we'll take four of those blueberry muffins, and I'll have a coffee."

"What kind of coffee?" Mallobarb snapped.

"What kind? Coffee coffee," he replied.

The line let out a collective groan, and Mrs. Finnegan could be heard muttering, "Amateurs."

"Get him the African blend," Briar said to her fairy godmothers.

They gave her a suspicious look, but rushed to fill the order. This gave the two adults a rare moment together without the watchful eyes of the rotund fairy chaperones.

"Any chance you could take a break?" Uncle Jake said.

"NO!" Everyone in the line shouted.

"We're in the middle of our lunchtime rush," Briar explained.

"Just a second," Uncle Jake pleaded, flashing a handsome grin at the princess.

Briar Rose laughed and then took off her apron. "Ladies, I'll be right back," she said as she tossed her apron on the counter.

The line turned on the Grimms. There was rage in their faces.

"People, try some decaf," Uncle Jake said. He opened the door wide, ushered the children out, and then bowed deeply as Briar Rose passed.

"Sorry about that," Briar said once they were outside. "Coffee is addictive, and people get angry when they need their fix."

"I've gotten warmer receptions from banshees," Uncle Jake said with a grin.

"At least Mallobarb and Buzzflower didn't try to turn you into a dung beetle this time," Briar replied.

"I told you I'd win them over."

Briar laughed. "I had a nice time last night."

"I'm still embarrassed about the meatball," Jake said, blushing.

"I had no idea they were so aerodynamic," Ms. Rose said with a giggle.

"I have to admit, I'm a bit of a klutz. If you keep seeing me, I'm going to ruin your entire wardrobe."

"Well, then you're lucky I like to shop," the princess said.

"Could someone kill me?" Puck begged. "If I have to hear one more word of this mushy love story, I'm going to throw myself off a bridge."

"Uh, I hate to admit it, but he's right. Aren't we supposed to be solving a mystery?" Sabrina said.

"Well, hello!" a voice said from behind them. The group turned around to find Tom Baxter crossing the street. He was with three young men, all wearing glasses and sweaters. Each wore a button pinned to his clothes that read I CALLED THE DR. CINDY SHOW. "Nice to see you again," the old man said with a smile.

"Nice to see you, too," Daphne said. "Where's Dr. Cindy?"

Tom pointed across the street to a tall building with a huge metal tower on its roof. Granny had once told Sabrina that it was the offices of Ferryport Landing's radio station, WFPR.

"She's busy preparing for tonight's show," Tom said. "It takes a lot of work and an awful lot of planning. But I'm being rude. Folks, these are some of my colleagues. Malcolm is our show's producer, Alexander is our sound engineer, and Bradford fields phone calls. They also help me cross the street from time to time."

Everyone introduced themselves and shook hands.

"I never miss a show," Puck said.

Sabrina turned, half expecting to find the boy laughing, but he was deadly serious.

"What?" Puck said defensively. "You should hear the people that call Dr. Cindy. All of them are sad, depressed, and lonely. It's one of the funniest shows on the radio."

Malcolm frowned. "Well, we better get our coffee and get back."

"He's right," Tom said. "Cindy can be a real bear when she doesn't get her latte."

The Grimms watched Tom and his coworkers enter the coffee shop, then they turned back to Ms. Rose.

"Briar, a few people at our party have had some things stolen from their homes," Uncle Jake said. "I don't want to pry, but if something were missing, we suspect it would be something magical. Have you or your fairy godmothers been robbed?"

"Mallobarb and Buzzflower don't let their magic wands out

of their sight, and all I have at home are a few magic seeds. Everything is accounted for."

"Perhaps I should come over some evening and just make sure," Uncle Jake said with a grin.

"You never quit, do you?" Ms. Rose said with a laugh. "Maybe you should ask Frau Pfefferkuchenhaus. Her office is right next door."

"Good idea. Kids, do you want to go do that?" Uncle Jake said, winking at them. Sabrina didn't have to be a mind reader to know he was trying to get a little alone time with the princess.

"Sure, we'll go take a look," Sabrina said, pulling her sister and Puck along. They walked next door and spotted a sign on the building that read DR. F. PFEFFERKUCHENHAUS—DENTIST. On the front door was a painting of several happy children with enormous, toothy smiles. All of them were saying, "Everyone smiles for Dr. P!" in a big cartoon balloon.

"What's a dentist?" Puck asked.

Sabrina cringed, imagining the cavities the boy must have. "There's a question you don't ever want to hear someone ask you."

The lobby was clean and neat, with paintings of dancing teeth all over the walls. A thin receptionist with eyeglasses that made her look like an owl sat at the desk filling out paperwork.

"Welcome to Dr. P's," she said when she looked up. Her glasses were so thick, Sabrina wondered if the woman might be able to see through her. "Do you have an appointment?"

"No, actually we were hoping we could talk to the doctor. Tell her that Sabrina and Daphne Grimm are here. She'll see us."

The receptionist picked up the phone and tapped a few buttons. "Dr. P, I'm sorry, I know you're with a patient. There are three children out here who say they know you. They say their last name is Grimm . . . really? Of course."

She hung up the phone and got up from her seat. "She'll see you."

She led the group through the hallway past several open doorways. As they walked past, Sabrina could see patients sitting in dental chairs getting their teeth cleaned. The high-pitched squeal of drills filled the air. Somewhere, a man let out a painful groan.

"Is this a torture chamber?" Puck asked eagerly. "Listen to all the suffering! Isn't it cool?"

"This is a dental office," the receptionist explained. "People come here to get a healthy smile."

There was another groan.

Puck laughed. "Sure! That guy sounds like he's smiling, all right! Are you hiring?"

The receptionist brought them to a room where they found

the gingerbread witch probing the teeth of a very nervous man in a chair. Sabrina had read the story of Hansel and Gretel and knew the witch's reputation, but at the same time she knew Frau P occasionally came to the family's assistance. Was she one of the good guys or a villain? Sabrina couldn't be sure. She had certainly never suspected that the woman's day job was dentistry. Hadn't she once had a house made out of candy?

"Mr. Easy, can you feel that?" she asked her patient. He had a suction tube in his mouth and Dr. P's fingers on his tongue.

The man said no, though with some difficulty.

"What about that?"

"No!"

"Good, and what about this one here?"

The man cried out in agony.

"OK, looks like you need some more gas," the witch said, covering Mr. Easy's face with a mask connected to a tank by a long tube. The man took several deep breaths and his tense hands relaxed their grip on the sides of his chair.

"Hello, Grimms. What can I do for you?" the witch said. "I'm having a special on root canals."

"We'll pass," Sabrina said. "We're investigating a series of crimes. Maybe you've heard about Morgan le Fay and Baba Yaga's problems?"

"Indeed I have," the witch said. "Let me finish up with Mr. Easy here, and I'll be right with you."

Dr. P picked up a tiny drill and turned it on. It whined loudly, and then she went to work on the poor man's teeth. The gas she had given him must have been wonderfully strong, as he barely even noticed the awful crunching noises.

Puck pushed his way in front of the girls to get a better view of the procedure. "I think I know what I want to be when I grow up," he said.

"Oh, there's lots of money in dentistry," the witch said over the noise. "People just can't get enough of the sugary sweets and they rarely floss. I've got appointments backed up for months."

"You mean, people pay you to do this to them? I thought you had captured these people and brought them here against their will. How do I become a dentist?"

"You have to go to school," Sabrina said, hoping the thought of an education might deter Puck's sudden career choice.

"You do?" the witch said, eyeing Sabrina. "I didn't know that."

Mr. Easy let out a groan, then mumbled something about seeing her medical license.

"What's that? You need more gas?" the witch said, shoving the mask back onto the man's face. Several seconds later he returned to la-la land. "I used to sell candy out of this place, but once the story got around, I couldn't drag children into the store."

"The Hansel and Gretel story?" Daphne said to clarify.

The witch nodded. "It ruined my business."

"Are you surprised?" Sabrina said.

"You did try to eat them," Daphne added.

"Oh, I did not!" the witch said, suddenly jerking and making a terrible cracking sound in Mr. Easy's mouth. "I was just trying to scare the little brats."

"That's not what I read," Sabrina said. She knew the story of Hansel and Gretel, two children who wandered into the woods and found a house made out of candy and gingerbread. The witch had captured the children and tried to fatten them up so she could devour them. It was gruesome stuff.

"Well, you shouldn't believe everything you read. First of all, those kids were out of control, wandering around in the woods, making all kinds of racket. I mean, what kind of parent lets their kids play in a forest? Really! People should have to have a license to have children.

"Second, they were eating my house," the witch continued as she went back to work on Mr. Easy's bicuspid. "The boy was outside gnawing on the fence, the girl was licking the shutters. Mongrels, that's what they were. I called the police and you know what they told me? If I was going to live in a house made of candy, I should expect children to come along and eat it. Is that what I was paying taxes for? No! So, I took the law into my own hands."

"You put them into a cage!" Sabrina said.

Puck laughed. "That's so awesome."

"It was only for a couple of hours. I fed them too, and trust me, it was the only decent meal the kids had had in a long time. Their mother never saw a carbohydrate she didn't love, and those kids were really packing on the pounds. That's the part of the story no one's ever heard. Yes, I fed them, but I gave them a salad. They had no idea what it was—apparently, they'd never had a meal that wasn't covered in cheese sauce! Well, after dinner I let them go and before I knew it I was being called a cannibal. The only thing bigger than their waistbands was their imagination."

The witch set her tools down and took off her rubber gloves. "Mr. Easy, I've got good news and bad news," she said to her patient, who gazed at her dreamily. "The good news is we're going to be able to save the bicuspid. The bad news: All the other teeth are going to have to come out."

"What?" Mr. Easy cried.

"You need more gas," Frau Pfefferkuchenhaus said as she took the mask and put it over her patient's mouth and nose. "Just breathe deep."

Mr. Easy's head was wobbly and a line of drool was dribbling down his chin. "Mughadinkalbeettershpliem," he mumbled.

The witch got up from her chair and led the children out into the hallway.

"We don't want to bother you, but we were wondering if anything has been stolen. Say, something magical?" Sabrina said.

The ancient witch shuffled uncomfortably and nodded. "I had a small vial of water from the Fountain of Youth."

"Why didn't *you* ever use it?" Puck asked rudely.

"It doesn't make you young," she replied with an angry glare.

"Uh, can we back up? What does this water do?" Daphne said.

"It stops you from getting any older. For an Everafter like me, it's worthless—we're immortal anyway—but I thought I might make a little extra cash someday selling what little I have to a human. Unfortunately, when I came in this morning, it was gone. Someone stole it right out of my locker."

"Could we take a look at the locker?" Sabrina asked.

The witch led the children down a hallway into a small room. There they found a table, some jackets hanging on the wall, and a row of lockers. One of the lockers had the door ripped off its hinges. It lay on the floor in a twisted heap.

"Whoever did it was strong enough to rip the door off," the witch said.

"No," Sabrina said, holding the warped locker door. "It pushed itself out from the inside. If someone had ripped it off, the bend would be going in the opposite direction."

She looked inside the locker and spotted the woman's handbag. There was a small hole in the side of it, identical to the one in Morgan le Fay's bag.

"So, you think whatever stole the water came out of this locker?" the witch said.

Sabrina nodded.

"Can you get the vial back for me?" the old witch continued.

"We're going to try," Sabrina said. "But maybe you can answer one more question. So far, the Wand of Merlin, the Wonder Clock, and your magic water are missing. Why would someone want those three things?"

Just then, the receptionist entered the room. "Dr. P, Mr. Easy is trying to escape."

"Give him some more gas and sit on him if you have to. I'll be right there," the witch said. When the receptionist raced back to the patient, the witch turned back to the children. "I can't honestly say. They're all pretty powerful items. Any one of them could cause havoc in the wrong hands. I wonder if the crooks are trying to use them all together."

"All together?" Sabrina said. "You can do that?"

"Sure. If you combine the properties of different magical items, you can create a brand-new kind of enchantment, though you'd have to be a pretty good sorcerer to make sure it didn't blow up in your face. Combining magical items can have unpredictable side-effects. Listen, I've got to run. The teeth don't pull themselves. If you find anything, let me know."

The witch darted down the hallway and left them alone.

"So, what have we learned?" Daphne asked, doing a funny impression of their grandmother's German accent. Then she pretended to get out a notebook and pen and jot down notes.

"I learned that you need no formal training to be a dentist!" Puck said.

"The Lilliputians and the mice are no longer suspects," Sabrina said. "Neither are strong enough to rip a steel locker door off its hinges. Unless they were on steroids."

"I'm lost," Daphne said. "Three break-ins, all done by something small and sneaky. We're going to have to go through the journals again."

The children exited the office and found their uncle and Briar Rose exactly where they had left them in front of the cafe.

"Any luck?" Uncle Jake asked when he finally noticed that they were waiting for him.

"A little, but we need to get home," Sabrina said.

The adults both frowned, but Uncle Jake eventually shrugged. He took the princess's hand and kissed it. "Until we meet again."

"OK, enough!" Puck cried. "If I have to, I'll turn a hose on you both."

Uncle Jake scowled. But before he could complain about them ruining his romantic moment, there was a terrible rumble, as if a tiny earthquake was erupting directly beneath the town. The tremors continued to grow in power, and then an explosion rattled the windows of the coffee shop. The noise had come from up the street. They all turned in that direction and found an unwelcome yet familiar sight. Baba Yaga and her house were stomping through town, in full view of humans. Worse, the witch was shooting buildings with fireballs emanating from one of her magic wands.

5

 want my property!" the witch shrieked.

"Briar, you might want to get to safety," Uncle Jake said as he began digging in his pockets.

"What about you?" Briar cried.

"Don't worry, I'm a Grimm. This is what we do."

Sabrina watched the princess run and wondered if she and her family should do the same. The witch was tearing through town, blasting one building after another. She screeched at the top of her lungs to be heard over the explosions and rumbling footsteps.

"Look at her!" Puck shouted. "She's horrible! She's like my soulmate!"

The house came to a stop outside the coffee shop and then bent down so that Uncle Jake's face and Baba Yaga's were a few feet apart. The witch breathed heavily and growled like an angry dog.

"Let me guess. You haven't had your coffee," Uncle Jake said. "I'll run in and get you one, and you'll feel better right away. How about a muffin to go with that? I hear the blueberry is to die for."

Baba Yaga shrieked again. "Have you got my wand, Grimm?"

Uncle Jake shook his head sheepishly.

"Then I will find it myself and woe to anyone who stands in my way."

"First, who uses the word 'woe' anymore?" Jake said. "Second, are you planning on burning the town down until someone confesses?"

Baba Yaga nodded. "Step aside, Jacob."

"No can do. You see, this store is owned by my would-be girlfriend. I can't let you burn it down. But if you have to destroy something, the tax assessor's office is just up the block."

Baba Yaga lifted her hands and a ball of fire appeared in them. It grew and grew and when it was as big as a beach ball, she wound up like a major-league pitcher.

"Uh-uh," Uncle Jake said. He took a small green amulet from one of his pockets and held it above his head. A light shot out of it and rose high into the air, then arced down and slammed into the ground as if it were more than particles or waves, but one solid, heavy mass. The ground shook and a tremor rose up like a mighty ocean wave, buckling the concrete and toppling Baba Yaga's house. The hut's hideous legs flailed as it tried desperately to right itself. Unfortunately, it wasn't long before it was back on its feet and stomping around angrily.

"What now?" Sabrina said.

"What do you mean 'what now'?" Uncle Jake said. "That should have taken care of her."

And then something happened that surprised even Baba Yaga—a thick black storm cloud appeared overhead. The wind swirled viciously, whipping across the street and ripping the awning off the front of Sacred Grounds. There was a flash of lightning and a loud explosion and then, as if they had stepped out of nowhere, a dozen men in loincloths and painted faces appeared. They were bare-chested and shoeless, and their skin was dark and tanned. A few held tomahawks in their hands, some had long spears, and others had bows and arrows. To Sabrina, they looked as if they had stepped out of the Native American exhibit at the Museum of Natural History.

The men scanned the area and seemed to understand that the house was a threat. They trained their weapons on Baba Yaga and shouted to one another in an odd, guttural language Sabrina couldn't understand.

One of the men bellowed and charged the house. The others followed, attacking with ferocious might. Their spears stabbed at the house's legs, causing it to hop up and down. Sabrina watched as Baba Yaga tried to cast a spell, most likely against the men, but with the house rocking back and forth so much, she couldn't keep her balance. Some of the men launched their arrows at the windows, and the witch had to dive out of the way to avoid being hit. A few of the arrows stuck into the sides of the house, and Sabrina sensed that the odd shack was in pain. Other men climbed the legs of the house, taking advantage of its confusion, and smashed their tomahawks into the walls. Pieces of wood splintered and fell to the ground.

"Nice work," Daphne said to their uncle.

"Uh, I didn't do this," Uncle Jake said, completely flabbergasted as he looked down at the little amulet. "At least, I don't think so."

Nottingham raced down the street with his dagger in hand. He came to a screeching halt when he spotted the strange scene in the middle of the road.

"Your little butter scraper isn't going to do much," Uncle Jake said to Nottingham as he pointed to the rows of burning buildings. "We've got a bigger problem now anyway. We need the Fire Department."

Nottingham's face turned red. "That's not possible."

"What? Why?" Sabrina demanded.

"The Fire Department was disbanded. The mayor had to make cuts and there wasn't room for them in the budget. Charming left us with quite a debt, you know."

"What are we going to do?" Sabrina yelled as the strange men fired another volley of arrows at Baba Yaga's shack.

"I'll handle it." Uncle Jake fumbled around in his pockets. He took out a golden ring, placed it on his hand, then rubbed it against his coat sleeve to shine the brilliant emerald at its center. He whispered something into it and it lit up like a brilliant firecracker. A moment later the sky emptied buckets of water down on everything. There was so much rain that Sabrina could barely see her sister to grab her hand. The rain swallowed up the flames, saving the town from imminent destruction.

When the rain slowed, Sabrina realized that the bizarre storm had vanished, along with the men and their weapons. All that was left was a bewildered Baba Yaga and her damaged home.

"I am not finished!" Baba Yaga cried as she craned her head out of one of her broken windows. "I'll be back!"

The house turned and stomped back down the street the way it came.

• • •

"Native Americans?" Granny Relda asked.

Uncle Jake nodded. "That's what they looked like to me."

Mr. Canis groaned. "And where are they now?"

"They vanished the way they came—into thin air," Uncle Jake said, examining his amulet.

"I wonder how Mayor Heart will clean up that mess without a coven of witches on her side. The Three used to take care of those kinds of things when Charming was in charge," Granny said.

"That's her problem now. We still have to deal with Baba Yaga," Mr. Canis replied. "The truth is, someone has to keep an eye on her. I should track her and make sure she doesn't get too close to the town."

"No," Granny Relda said. "Jacob will take care of that."

"Me?" Uncle Jake cried. "She threatened to eat me once."

"I'll go with you," Puck said. "I'm learning a lot from the old witch."

"Fine. Mr. Canis, I was hoping you would look after the girls," Granny suggested.

"What about the case?" Daphne said.

Granny shook her head. "*Liebling*, I'm afraid we're going to have to put detective work on hold. There are too many emergencies to deal with, and we can't be everywhere at the same time."

"But—" Sabrina started, but her grandmother threw up her hands.

"We just can't. Now, I have to get ready. Ms. White has agreed to take me to the bank. I'm applying for a loan to pay our taxes."

Everyone darted off in his or her own direction, leaving Sabrina and Daphne alone with Mr. Canis, who didn't look at all happy to be stuck with the girls.

"So . . . ," Sabrina said as she eyed the old man. His upper fangs had started to creep down his lips.

"So," he huffed.

"You're babysitting us, huh?"

Mr. Canis raised his eyebrows, acknowledging his new role.

"Want to play a game?" Daphne asked. "We've got Candy Land."

Mr. Canis shifted uncomfortably.

"No!" Daphne cried as she jumped to her feet. "I know what we can do. We can play dress-up!"

Sabrina couldn't help but laugh.

"Perhaps we should continue with our tracking lessons," Mr. Canis said to the girls. "Put on your boots. We still have a few hours of daylight."

Mr. Canis led them around the back of the house and deep into the woods. The ground was muddy and there was still a chill in the air, but little buds were sprouting on tree limbs. Sabrina couldn't remember the last time she saw something growing, but soon spring would be in full bloom. Sabrina wondered what the forest would look like when it was fresh and alive.

They climbed along a small ravine and up a hill littered with sharp stones, then down into a gulch. A tiny creek trickled along with shards of ice floating on top of it.

"Are we about to lose the house?" Daphne asked the old man.

"Your grandmother is a resourceful woman," Mr. Canis said.

"That's not an answer," Sabrina said. She didn't want to anger the old man, which had become increasingly easy to do, but she needed him to be honest with them.

"She will not let you down, girls. In the time I have known her, she has never failed or disappointed. I trust her. You should as well."

"Three hundred thousand dollars is a lot of money," Sabrina pointed out.

"Yes, it is," the old man replied. "Fortunately, this situation will benefit you in your training. Stress is an enemy. It confuses us and makes us question ourselves. The calm, rational mind is the one that finds answers in difficult times. Remember, you will not always have the carefree lives of children, but you will always be Grimms and you will have to find ways to set aside private matters."

"So you want us to forget about the tax bill?" Daphne said.

"The three-hundred-thousand-dollar tax bill?" Sabrina added.

Mr. Canis took an impatient breath. "Close your eyes."

The girls did as they were told.

"In the past we have tracked deer and rabbits, as well as the family dog. You've learned to follow and recognize the prints of many wild animals. Today, you will follow the prints of the most dangerous animal of all—me. I will hide from you in this forest and you will have to use your senses and what I have taught you to find me. Your grandmother has achieved great skill at this with practice, and she uses these talents quite frequently. Remember—use your senses. Learn to trust what you see, smell, hear, and feel. Allow them to work together and you two should have no problem locating me."

"I've got a question," Daphne said.

There was no response.

"Mr. Canis?"

Sabrina opened her eyes. The old man was gone. She pinched Daphne softly and the little girl looked around.

"Well, that was mucho rude-o," Daphne complained.

Sabrina scanned the dense woods. Canis was nowhere in sight, but he had left a trail in the snow. Following it wouldn't be too difficult—after all, in his semialtered form Mr. Canis had what amounted to size-22 shoes.

Sabrina pointed to the tracks. "He went that way."

The girls followed the footprints through some heavy brush. The old man's path showed he was running in one direction and then cutting back in the other, obviously trying to confuse them.

"Are we really going to have to live in a refrigerator box like Puck said?" Daphne asked. "I don't think we'll all fit in a refrigerator box. Mr. Canis won't for sure, and what about Elvis? I guess we could get a washing machine box for him. We could even decorate it and cut out some windows."

The little girl rambled on, describing how with a little creativity they could turn an old cardboard box into a two-story Colonial, while Sabrina led her along the trail Mr. Canis had left. It took them up a steep climb, but they found a couple of branches that doubled as walking sticks that helped their ascent. At the top of the crest they found more trees, but Mr. Canis's footprints had disappeared.

"Where did he go?" Daphne asked.

"Maybe he's soaking in our cardboard-box Jacuzzi," Sabrina replied.

"OK, fine, I'll concentrate," Daphne grumbled. "It's just I wish I had a magic wand or a crystal ball."

Sabrina scanned the area but saw nothing. He couldn't have just vanished into thin air, but . . .

"Look!" Sabrina said, pointing up at the trees. She saw dozens of limbs splintered and broken, with fresh yellow wood erupting from their rich brown bark. "He jumped up there and grabbed those branches. They snapped when he swung to the next tree."

"I thought he was a wolf, not a monkey."

Sabrina scanned the next tree and saw a similar limb. "Then he swung over there."

"See!" Daphne said. "You're mucho excellent-o at tracking."

Sabrina swelled with pride. Her sister was right. She was good at tracking. "Thanks," Sabrina said as she pointed toward a row of trees. "He went that way."

The girls held hands and continued through the woods. It dawned on Sabrina that this was what Puck must have done when he was stalking them during escape training. He used their environment against the girls, finding the little clues their feet and bodies left behind. With a keen eye, the woods could become like a road map leading them to their destination.

It wasn't long before they found another set of Mr. Canis's footprints that led to a churning brook. There his trail ended. Sabrina studied the banks of the stream and searched the trees but saw nothing.

"What now?"

"Close your eyes," Sabrina told her sister. "He told us to use all our senses."

She stood quietly, trying to sort through the noises around her: the bubbling water, the creaky branches swaying in the breeze, a bird chirping high in the trees. And then she heard it: A twig snapped in the brush nearby.

"He's in there," Sabrina said, pulling her sister along. They pushed through the bushes, even getting on their hands and knees to crawl through. It wasn't easy and the girls were filthy, but that was the least of their worries. Without warning the gray sky had filled with dark clouds and a storm swirled above. A crack of thunder shook the trees and bolts of lightning burst out of a black hole in the sky. It looked just like the storm that had occurred when the odd men had attacked Baba Yaga, and the one on the night Sabrina had imagined Uncle Jake's death.

"Maybe we should call it a day," Sabrina said as she examined the troubling storm. She turned to crawl back the way they came. Once through the bushes, she struggled to her feet and helped her sister do the same.

"Mr. Canis!" Daphne shouted. "We're going home!"

"A storm is coming!" Sabrina shouted. "Can you hear us, Mr. Canis?"

"I don't know if Canis can hear you," a growling voice said from within the bushes, "but I certainly can."

Sabrina studied the brush, trying to find the source of the strange, yet familiar voice. She heard rough laughter that seemed to come at them from all sides. Finally she spotted a pair of eyes peering back at her, and then a monstrous figure pushed forward, uprooting an unfortunate tree that was in its way. When the creature was out in the open, Sabrina nearly screamed. Standing before her was a wolf as big as a grizzly bear, though it stood on its two back legs like a man. It snarled and snapped at Sabrina as it looked over the girls curiously.

"The Wolf," Daphne gasped.

The girls stumbled backward and fell to the ground. Sabrina's mind was reeling. What had happened to cause Mr. Canis to lose control of himself? Why had he let the Big Bad Wolf loose?

The Wolf stomped forward, shoving its snout into Daphne's face and blasting her with a foul spray.

"Don't try to run, girlie!" the Wolf said as he snatched Daphne by her coat and lifted her off the ground. "You'll just build up my appetite."

Sabrina was terrified, but she couldn't let her sister be hurt. She leaped to her feet and rushed at the Wolf with her fists clenched. She was met with a painful backhand that sent her slamming into the ground. Her shoulder fell hard on a stone. She cried out and forced herself to stand. Her arm didn't feel broken, but the pain was excruciating. She knew fighting was pointless. *The Wolf is too big and strong, but I have to do something.* She spotted a sharp black rock on the ground, snatched it up, aimed, and flung it as hard as she could. It hit the Wolf and bounced off his chest like she had tossed a peanut at him.

"Was that supposed to hurt?" He laughed.

"No!" a voice said from behind Sabrina. "But I bet this will!"

A flaming rocket blasted past Sabrina and hit the Wolf squarely in the chest. He howled and fell backward, releasing Daphne, who tumbled to the ground. Sabrina rushed to her sister's side and dragged her away, then turned to find out who had saved them. Two women were standing behind her. One was tall and fierce with long blond hair and a deadly looking sword in her hands, as well as an array of weapons strapped around her waist and legs, including daggers, grenades, and a whip. The other woman had dark brown hair and wore a long trench coat that had hundreds of extra pockets sewn into it. It looked just like Uncle Jake's coat. The brown-haired woman was also adorned with necklaces and jeweled rings, one of which was glowing. Her expression was stern and serious, like hardened steel. She was beautiful, but her face was marred by a horrible scar.

"You're not going to touch them, mutt," the blond woman said, waving her sword in the air.

"Or someone is going to get fixed," the woman in the coat added.

The Wolf clambered to his feet and eyed the women. "Back off. These are my kills!"

"You back off, or I'll take your other eye," the woman with the sword replied. It was then that Sabrina noticed that the Wolf's left eye was white with blindness and framed by an ugly scar.

The monster growled and leaped at the blond woman. She swung her sword and hit the beast in the arm. The Wolf shrieked and swung back, hitting her so hard she flew against a tree. The brunette rubbed the glowing ring against her jacket and another blast rocketed at the monster. The Wolf leaped out of the way, dodging the projectile by inches.

The woman with the sword sprang to her feet. With the Wolf in pain and confused, she climbed up onto his enormous back. Raising her weapon high over his head, she brought the hilt down hard between the beast's eyes. He staggered, dazed. "He's all yours, sister," she shouted to her companion.

The dark-haired woman pulled a wand from inside her coat. She flicked her wrist and said, "Gimme some chains," and a ray of light shot out of the wand's tip. The woman's aim was perfect

and a stream of particles fluttered out of the wand, forming a chain so thick it looked as if it could tie down a battleship. The chains themselves weaved around the Wolf, binding him tightly. He struggled, snarling and snapping at the women, but he was momentarily helpless.

"Who are they?" Daphne whispered to her sister.

Sabrina searched her memory for any reference to a couple of tough chicks who could take down the Big Bad Wolf. She'd never read anything in the family journals about them. "I was hoping you would know."

The blond woman turned to Sabrina and looked at her closely. Suddenly her confident face turned pale, as if she had just seen a ghost. "It can't be . . . ," she began, but she didn't get to finish. The Wolf broke loose from the chains with a powerful shrug. He pounced forward, slamming into the women and knocking them both to the ground.

"I've been waiting a long time for this meal," the Wolf said, licking his huge jaws.

"Uh-uh-uh," said a voice from above them. It was deep but had a playful, boyish quality. Sabrina looked up and saw a man with golden hair descending from the trees. On his back were a pair of huge insectlike wings. "I hate it when people threaten my family. It's so . . . well, rude."

An arrow flew from the crossbow in his hands. It hit the Wolf in the leg and the monster bellowed, crashing to the ground. The fairy attacked again, his head morphing into that of a saber-toothed tiger. He sunk his heavy fangs into the monster's back and the Wolf shrieked.

"We need to go get help," Sabrina said to her sister. She snatched the little girl by the sleeve and pulled her into the woods, leaving the battle behind.

"But the house is back the other way," Daphne cried.

"We're not going to the house," Sabrina said. "Granny's at the bank, and so is our secret weapon."

6

he girls hurried through the woods, clambering over rocks and down hills until they finally found a road. It was there that Daphne pulled away to catch her breath.

"We should go back home and get Uncle Jake," the little girl said.

"He's not there, remember?" Sabrina said. "Everyone is out running errands."

"But what about those women and the fairy? We can't just leave them back there. He'll kill them," Daphne argued.

"I think the three of them can defend themselves," Sabrina said as she scanned the edge of the forest in case the Wolf had indeed slaughtered the odd trio and was now on their trail. "Besides, we're just a couple of kids. We need help if we're going to try to stop Mr. Canis."

"What kind of help?"

Sabrina approached her sister. "You remember the key that Mr. Hamstead gave us before we left New York City?"

Daphne slipped a hand inside of her shirt and pulled out a necklace. Dangling from its end was a small silver key with several numbers engraved on its side. "This?"

Sabrina nodded. "Remember, Hamstead gave us this and told us to use it only if Mr. Canis ever lost control of the Wolf. It opens a safety-deposit box. Hamstead said there was a weapon inside that could stop the Wolf in his tracks."

Daphne looked down at the silver key. "What's a safety-deposit box?"

"It's like a safe. You put your valuables in it. They keep them at the bank."

"That's where Granny is."

"I know. She can help us too." Sabrina took Daphne's hand. "We have to hurry."

Unfortunately the road they were on was the long way to town, and it took several hours of steady walking before they came across any hint of civilization. The first thing they recognized was a farm they had driven by many times. Granny had told them it was owned by Old McDonald, the farmer from the famous nursery rhyme. But as they approached, they were shocked to see that the farm looked as if it had been abandoned. The fields were overgrown with weeds, the barns were falling down on themselves, and the cattle pens and livestock houses were empty. As they got closer they realized that the farmer's house had been destroyed by a terrible fire. Oddly, the destruction appeared to have occurred long ago.

"What happened?" Daphne said, asking the question Sabrina had knocking around in her own head.

"I don't know," Sabrina said. "Did Granny mention this?"

Daphne shook her head.

"C'mon," Sabrina continued. "We can't hang out here all day. I think we've got another half an hour of walking before we get to Main Street."

They soon came across the rusty railroad tracks that ran along the Hudson River and led to the train station in the center of town. As they walked along the tracks they saw more surprising scenes. The stern of an enormous sunken ship was sticking out of the water. Several broken-down cars lined the grassy beach. When they finally stepped into town, they noticed a sign above the train station. It had once read WELCOME TO FERRYPORT LANDING, but someone had crossed out the FERRYPORT and added a more sinister message. The sign now read BEWARE! YOU ARE NOW ENTERING *FAIRY*PORT LANDING!

Even more shocking was the state of the town. The little shops were abandoned, their doors torn away and windows broken. Many stores were in flames. There were sounds of fire alarms in the distance, but no sign of any fire trucks. The streets were deserted, riddled with potholes and smoldering automobiles.

Sabrina couldn't believe what she was seeing. "I guess Uncle Jake isn't doing such a good job of keeping Baba Yaga in check."

"This is going to take an awful lot of Forgetful Dust," Daphne said as she gaped at all the destruction.

When they came upon the bank, they were stunned to find the building was nothing but cinders. Everything inside it was burned to a black ash, including the tellers' windows, the ATM, and most important, the safety-deposit boxes. There was nothing left.

"Granny!" Daphne cried, nearly in hysterics.

Sabrina reached down and scooped up a handful of ash. It was cool to the touch.

"Daphne, this happened a long time ago," Sabrina said, trying to reassure her sister while deciphering the puzzle before her. "If the bank burned down this morning, why is the ash cold?"

Sabrina looked around at the little town. The streets were empty. In fact, there wasn't a living soul in sight. Where were all the people?

"Something's wrong," she said. "I must be having another hallucination."

"Well, I'm having the same one you are," Daphne said.

Suddenly, the street went dark, as if something had blocked out the sun. Sabrina watched an enormous shadow zip across the street and vanish. The sunshine returned as fast as it disappeared.

"Uh, what was that?" Daphne said nervously.

Sabrina scanned the skies. "Must have been a cloud."

Just then, there was an enormous roar, like the angry threats of a thousand lions. It rattled Sabrina's ears as well as a loose shard of glass in the window of Dr. P's abandoned dentist office. The glass fell from its frame and broke on the pavement.

"Clouds don't make noises like that," Daphne said. "Clouds don't make noises at all!"

Sabrina continued studying the sky. She spotted something far off on the horizon. At first it was tiny—no bigger than a bird—but as it approached, Sabrina could see that it was actually quite large and incredibly fast. As it drew closer, Sabrina could make out its bright red wings, which spanned the width of a football field. They supported a huge, reptilian body covered in scales and a long tail that slashed through the air. The creature's neck was snakelike and it had enormous teeth. Sabrina had seen a drawing of it in an old children's book. She had even seen a movie about a kid who had one as a pet. But this thing was no pet.

"Run!" Sabrina yelled as she latched onto her sister's hand. Together they sped down the broken street, dodging potholes and burned-out cars.

"Sabrina, is that what I think it is?" Daphne shouted over the monster's wail.

And then the creature fell from the sky and landed in their path. It crouched down, almost like a cat, and sniffed the air around them. Its breath smelled of fumes and sulfur.

"Yes. It's a dragon," Sabrina whispered.

The creature roared once more and a blast of blisteringly hot air danced across Sabrina's skin. Luckily the beast was too far away to burn them.

"Heads up, kiddies!" said a voice from above. Sabrina looked to the sky, sure that the voice belonged to their only hope— Puck. But it wasn't Puck. Instead, it was the strange fairy they had encountered in the woods. He fell out of the sky like a missile and planted his feet on top of the dragon's snout. The impact forced the beast's chin into the pavement, stunning it for a few moments. Then it reared back and belched a ball of flame at the fairy. The winged man was quick in the air, darting back and forth with amazing speed and agility, and the deadly missile never reached its target. But the dragon was not discouraged. It let loose a dozen more blasts at the flying man, edging closer to him with each attempt. Luckily, the fairy steered the monster away from Sabrina and Daphne.

"You have to come with us," said a voice from behind them. The girls spun around to find the blond warrior woman. She had her sword drawn, while her sister, the dark-haired woman, was holding a wand that glowed with green energy.

"We're not going anywhere with you," Sabrina said, stepping in front of her sister. She clenched her fists and snarled, preparing for a fight if the older women wanted one. She set her feet the way Ms. White had taught her, but before she could even take a swing, the fairy snatched her and Daphne off the ground and hoisted them onto his shoulders like they were a couple of sacks of potatoes.

"There's no time to explain," the fair-haired woman said. "We have to get to safety. If they find you out here, they will kill you."

"Who?" Daphne cried. "Who will kill us?"

"The Scarlet Hand."

Sabrina and Daphne shouted a million questions, but every one was ignored. Instead, the dark-haired woman reached into one of the many pockets on her jacket and took out what appeared to be a tiny blue marble. With her other hand she snatched Sabrina by the arm. The blond woman grabbed Sabrina by the other arm and then latched onto Daphne.

"Don't forget about me," the fairy said as he planted a kiss on the blond woman and put an arm around her waist. A moment later Sabrina felt energy swirl around her body. It seemed to invade her pores, rush through her bloodstream, and dance on the edges of her mind. She looked over at her sister to find that Daphne's hair was standing on end, and she had to assume her own was doing the same. There was a bright flash of light, like someone was snapping a picture, and then Sabrina felt a far more peculiar sensation. It wasn't uncomfortable or painful, but it felt as if her body was being folded neatly into halves, then folded again, and again, and again, until she was a tiny fragment of herself—so small she was invisible—and then she was folded once more and vanished from existence.

• • •

When the lights came on, Sabrina found herself lying on a pile of rags in a filthy room. Scattered about were musty books, old furniture, and boxes of odd trinkets. She scanned the room, puzzled by its familiarity. She had been here before, but where was here? She looked up at the filthy chandelier and then at a table covered in potions and odd books. One of them she could clearly see was bound with what looked like human skin. She fought a wave of revulsion.

"We're inside Baba Yaga's house," Sabrina croaked.

"What?" Daphne said groggily. The little girl was lying right next to Sabrina. "I was having a dream about ice cream."

"Do you know how we got here?" Sabrina asked.

Daphne shook her head.

"It's really freaky," a voice said from behind them. Sabrina spun around to find the grown-up fairy sitting on a chair, watching over them. "When is your birthday?"

"It's in two days," Sabrina replied suspiciously. "I'll be twelve."

Just then, the warrior sisters entered the room. Sabrina studied them, noticing the scar that ran along the dark-haired woman's face. It started at the bottom of her earlobe and ran down to just below her chin. It was an ugly wound and from what Sabrina could tell, fairly fresh.

"I don't remember this happening," the fairy said to the women. "But then again, you two were always running off on your own back then. Did it happen and you just didn't tell me?"

The blond woman shook her head. "This definitely did not happen."

"It appears as if the phenomenon has occurred again," the woman with the scar replied.

"What are you talking about?" Sabrina demanded. "What phenomenon?"

"We should take them to William," the dark-haired woman said, ignoring Sabrina's questions.

"We should take them as far away from here as possible," her sister argued. "Who knows what could happen if they got hurt."

"You need to take us home," Sabrina interrupted. "Everything has gone crazy. The town is in ruins, there are dragons flying around, and Mr. Canis has lost control of himself. I know he looks like a monster, but that thing you were fighting is our friend."

The brown-haired woman's face looked tense. "That creature is no one's friend," she said sternly. "We barely got away with our lives."

"You don't understand," Sabrina argued. "My family can help. We fix problems all the time. You need to let us go home."

"I'm afraid we can't do that," the blond woman said.

"Oh yeah? Who do you think you are, kidnapping us?"

The blond woman reached out for a handshake. "My name is Sabrina Grimm. This is my sister, Daphne Grimm, and my husband, Puck."

Sabrina and Daphne stared at them.

"You people are nutballs!" Sabrina cried.

"Mucho nutballs-o!"

The woman claiming to be Daphne ignored the insult. "House, head for the mountains!" she shouted, and the house made an abrupt turn, jostling the girls until they both fell to the floor. If there had been any lingering doubt in Sabrina's mind that they were in Baba Yaga's home, it was now gone.

The blond woman who called herself Sabrina helped Sabrina and Daphne back to their feet. "I'm guessing that you're pretty confused, but we'll sort this out as soon as we get back to the camp."

"What camp?"

Again, their questions were ignored and the house marched on, thumping and bouncing with every step. Sabrina couldn't be sure, but she felt as if it might be running at a full sprint.

• • •

The camp was really a fortress surrounded by high walls made of logs. It was built in the shape of a square, with four tall towers at each corner. The towers had lookouts and each was equipped with a large cannonlike weapon that had water dripping from its barrel. Long hoses ran out of the back of the weapons and down the inside of the walls. Sabrina watched from a window of Baba

Yaga's house as an immense gate swung open to allow them to enter the compound. Once the witch's house was inside, the gate was closed again and then reinforced with beams to prevent it from being opened from outside.

Inside stood a dozen tiny cabins made from stones, a small farm, a pen for cattle and chickens, and what looked like an elaborate obstacle course. Men and women rushed through it while a small man barked orders at them.

The house trotted over to a well and awkwardly dropped to the ground. Sabrina noticed the long tubes attached to the cannons ran down into the well, and she understood that the weapons in the towers shot water, probably at approaching dragons.

A moment later, the fairy who claimed to be Puck opened the door. Waiting outside was an elderly man wearing what appeared to be a burlap sack he had fashioned into a shirt and pants.

"How goes it, Faithful John?" the fairy asked, taking the man's hand and shaking it vigorously.

"All is quiet, so all is good," the man said with a smile.

"Where's William?" the woman with the scar asked as she stepped outside.

"He's on patrol but should be back soon," Faithful John replied. Just then, there was a loud trumpeting. "I guess that's him."

The doors swung open once more and a great white horse charged through. A rugged man, dressed in purple slacks and a white shirt, sat atop the horse. His hair was long and dark and he held a sword in one hand and the horse's reins in the other. Sabrina and Daphne had to jump out of the horse's path for fear of being trampled.

"The Hand has a platoon of card soldiers by the river!" the man shouted. "Tell the general that we might be able to attack at dusk."

Faithful John nodded and raced toward a tent on the other side of the camp.

As for the man on the horse, he leaped off while the great doors of the camp were once again secured. Sabrina took a closer look at him. He was shockingly handsome, despite his unkempt beard, long hair, and filthy clothing. There was also something very familiar about him, though she couldn't be sure just what.

The man sensed her looking and turned and stared at the girls for a long moment. Then, without warning, he wrapped them up in his arms and cried with happiness.

"Girls! How did you get here?"

Sabrina pulled herself away. "Uh, hello, personal space!"

"It's me. Prince Charming!"

"Nuh-uh," Daphne said, but Sabrina wasn't so sure. She studied his face using her imagination to cut his hair and shave his beard. It didn't make sense, but soon it was clear that the man was telling the truth.

"Where did you come from?" he asked, reaching out and shaking them happily.

"We were out in the woods with Mr. Canis and—"

"Canis! Is he here too?" the prince said hopefully. Sabrina had never heard Charming speak of their family friend with anything but disdain.

"You have to help us," Sabrina said, struggling to believe that she was asking the notoriously grouchy prince for his assistance. "These freaks kidnapped us before I could warn Granny and Uncle Jake about what is going on."

"Yeah, the town has gone mucho crazy-o!" Daphne said.

The former mayor's face sank. "No. No! No! No!" he said as he shook his head.

"Charming, we have to do something. Mr. Canis has turned into the Big Bad Wolf and there are dragons everywhere. The whole town is in danger."

"You don't have to worry about Mr. Canis. Everyone's better off where they are," Charming said as he ran his hand through his dusty hair. "In the past."

"Not you, too!" Sabrina groaned. "I've had it with this practical joke. What do you want me to say? I believe you? You've fooled me? Well, forget it. It takes a lot to pull a prank on me."

"It's not a prank," the blond warrior said. "Ferryport Landing has been like this for almost fifteen years."

"That's impossible!" Sabrina exclaimed as she felt her sister slip her hand into her own and squeeze tightly.

"Sabrina," the woman continued. "I'm you. I'm twenty-six years old. In two days I'll be twenty-seven." She turned to the dark-haired woman she called her sister. "And this is Daphne."

Sabrina studied their faces. She had to admit the dark-haired woman did look like Daphne, but without all the light and happiness of her sister's face.

"And I'm Puck," the fairy said. His big pink wings popped out of his back and lifted him several feet off the ground. He put his hands on his hips and grinned broadly. "Taa-daa!"

"Now I know this is a joke," Sabrina said, spinning on the fairy. "Everafters don't grow old."

"Not true, Sabrina. An Everafter can grow old if he wants. Most don't because they don't have a good reason," Puck said, sharing an affectionate look with the woman claiming to be Sabrina. The fairy had a gold ring on his left hand that was identical to one the older Sabrina wore.

Daphne squealed. "You mean . . . you and Puck . . . really . . . married!"

The older Sabrina grinned bashfully, then looked at the fairy. "He gets a little less annoying as he gets older."

"But only a little," the fairy said with a laugh. He rubbed the top of Sabrina's head. "We should introduce our guests to the general."

They walked to a tent at the center of the camp. Charming pulled back the flaps and ushered the girls inside. The older versions of themselves and Puck followed. Inside, Sabrina saw a queen-size bed. Two adults lay on top of it, sound asleep.

"Mom! Dad!" the girls cried, and rushed to their side.

"They're still asleep," a voice said from behind them. It was old and crackling, but oddly familiar. Sabrina turned around and saw an old woman in a wheelchair in the door of the tent.

"Girls, I'd like to introduce you to the general," Charming said.

Sabrina studied the woman closely. She wore a bright yellow dress and a matching hat with a sunflower appliqué at its center. Trotting around her chair were four Great Dane puppies. She was incredibly old, but her eyes still had a youthful glimmer.

"Granny Relda!" Daphne cried as she raced across the room and wrapped the old woman in a hug. Sabrina followed more slowly, shocked at how old Granny looked.

"There's a name I haven't heard in many years," the old woman said. She studied the girls' faces and then turned to their older counterparts with a confused expression.

"It's a long story, old lady," Puck said.

"Well, I suppose you better start telling it," Granny replied.

• • •

The group shared a meal of potatoes, venison, and black bread while the recent events were explained to the future version of Granny Relda. During the meal she studied maps and reports provided to her by soldiers who waited for her orders, then ran off to perform their duties. Sabrina watched the old woman closely, noticing the deep lines in her face and the trembling, arthritic hands.

Some time during the meal, a little man wearing a crude military uniform emblazoned with dozens of bright badges and medals came over to the table. He was the same man they had spotted training soldiers. He saluted the old woman with great respect. They briefly discussed the forces at the riverside and agreed on the best strategy for attack. When the conversation was over, he saluted Granny Relda again and then disappeared. It took Sabrina several minutes to realize who he was.

"That was Mr. Seven!" Daphne said.

"Actually, we call him Captain Seven," Granny Relda replied.

"Captain Seven is a great leader and demands quite a bit of respect around here," Charming explained. "He's been responsible for many of our army's successes."

"Why do you need an army?" Sabrina asked.

"To fight the Scarlet Hand, of course," Granny said as she tossed chunks of her dinner to her four impatient puppies. "Since the Master rose, we've been one of the main fronts in the battle for human freedom. There are other units scattered around the world, and I've been leading the charge. That's how I got my little nickname. Truth is, without Seven and the brave members of the army we wouldn't stand a chance. The Master and his Hand are relentless."

"But how did it get this bad?" Daphne asked as she glanced around at the rough camp.

"They plundered the Hall of Wonders," the grown-up Sabrina explained. "They opened every door and took anything of value. What they didn't take, they set free. There were horrible things behind some of those doors. It threw the town into chaos."

She shared a knowing look with the old woman.

"One of them tried to barbeque you earlier today," Puck added.

"Why didn't we stop it from happening?" Sabrina wondered.

"What were we supposed to do, Sabrina?" Granny Relda said,

before breaking into a coughing fit. When she recovered, she continued. "What could an old woman and two little girls do?"

"You're forgetting Elvis," Daphne said.

"And we must not do that. He was a brave soul. These four pups are his great-grandchildren. Let me introduce you to John, Paul, George, and Ringo."

The dogs raced over to Daphne and sat with begging eyes until the girl surrendered her venison steak.

"Yep, they're related," Daphne said as she hugged them all.

"What about Uncle Jake?"

The old woman shifted sadly in her chair.

"He was arrested and put into the Ferryport Prison," she said softly. "They gave him a trial and sentenced him to life, but he tried to escape and he was killed."

"I saw it!" Sabrina cried. "I saw that happen outside our window. He was shot with an arrow."

Granny Relda shared a confused expression with the older women and Puck. "I don't remember that happening."

"I certainly don't remember it," the grown-up Sabrina replied. "How can these things have occurred in the past but we don't remember them? Our Prince Charming didn't disappear. I never saw Uncle Jake murdered when I was young. We didn't just pop up in the future, either."

"How long have you been here?" Charming asked the girls.

"A couple of hours," Sabrina said. "What about you?"

"Three months."

"So, you're not a future version of Prince Charming?" Sabrina asked, doing her best to understand all the new information.

"No, I'm from the past—I mean, the present . . . it's all still very confusing. I went for a walk after I lost the election to the Queen of Hearts. I wanted to clear my head, think of a way to change my fortunes, and then I found myself here. It took me several hours to figure out that I wasn't where I was supposed to be. It appears the same thing has happened to the two of you."

The older Daphne shook her head. "Something is happening back then that shouldn't have happened," she said. "We believe it's creating tears in time."

"Tears in time?" Daphne asked.

"Yes, they're doorways that suck people out of their time. They're not supposed to be possible, but whatever or whoever is causing them is somehow blending their future and our present."

"And maybe all of our pasts," Sabrina interrupted. "We saw a band of Indians attack Baba Yaga this afternoon. I mean, fifteen years ago."

"Now, I *know* that never happened," the older Daphne said.

"So this is worse than I suspected," Granny Relda replied.

"When the two of you vanished, did you see a storm come out of nowhere?" Charming asked.

Sabrina nodded. "And there was one when I saw Uncle Jake die."

"And when the Indians appeared and attacked Baba Yaga," Daphne added. "By the way, where is she?"

"The witch was one of the first of the resistance to die," Granny Relda said. "She made a foolish error when she destroyed her guardians. She never took time to replace them and it left her vulnerable. The Scarlet Hand cornered her in the forest and killed her, but not before she took out nearly forty of them."

"The house ran off," Puck said. "We found it cowering at the top of Mount Taurus and we've been using it ever since."

"Maybe all this has something to do with the case we're working on," Sabrina said, watching the older version of her sister standing cold and distant, away from the group. She shuddered to think what had happened to steal the happiness from Daphne, or what had caused the horrible mark on her face.

"What case?" Granny Relda asked.

"Someone's been stealing magic items. The Wand of Merlin, the Wonder Clock, and some water from the Fountain of Youth have all been ripped off."

"I remember that case," Granny Relda said. "We never solved it."

"Unbelievable! Relda Grimm would never let a mystery go unsolved," Charming said with a hint of disdain.

"There were other things, urgent things that needed our attention," the old woman said.

"The taxes," Sabrina asked.

Her older self nodded in agreement. "Yes, among others. Uncle Jake had his hands full with Baba Yaga. After that, things got even worse and we just never had time to do any more investigating."

"What got worse?" Sabrina asked, suspiciously.

The adults were silent for a long, heartbreaking moment. They looked at one another with strained expressions, as if weighing how much pain their next words might cause.

"They should see the house," the older Daphne said.

"Don't you think that's a little harsh?" Granny Relda asked.

"If we don't show them the truth, they will go and discover it for themselves. You remember how we used to be. We were always running off in the middle of the night. We can't allow them to do that. They wouldn't survive. It's best if we feed their curiosity, no matter how painful it may be."

"She's right, Relda," Charming said. "They'll sneak out, and this time, they might not come back."

"If they were to be killed, we would die with them. They're us," the grown-up Daphne added.

The older Sabrina shrugged. "I guess it's for the best."

Sabrina and Daphne stared into each other's eyes. Silently, they shared their fear for what they were about to see. What could be so bad?

"Show us," Sabrina said.

• • •

Sabrina felt the house make another abrupt turn. She glanced out the window and saw abandoned homes and a forest charred with black smoke. Roads were ripped in half and littered with abandoned cars.

After a while, the creepy shack came to a lumbering stop.

"We're here," the future Daphne said as she glanced through the window. "We can't stay long."

"The dragons circle the area in fifteen-minute cycles and we don't know when the last one started," Granny Relda explained.

Sabrina felt the house lower. The older Puck came from the other room with his crossbow and arrows in hand. He kicked open the door, took a peek outside, and then gestured for everyone to follow. Sabrina and Daphne shuffled outside with Charming close behind.

And then they saw it, the plot of land that had been their grandmother's home. Their house and any sign that it had ever existed was gone. Not even the trees had been left behind. Instead, an enormous castle made from black stones sat on the property. It had two high towers and a drawbridge over a moat dug around the perimeter of the building. On top of one of the towers, a black flag with a bloodred handprint in its center fluttered in the wind. The air smelled of sulfur.

Sabrina could feel tears run down her face, and for the first time in her life she didn't try to hide them.

"I haven't been here in fifteen years," the old Sabrina said. "Never thought I'd be strong enough to look out at it—"

"How do we fix this?" Sabrina interrupted.

"Fix it?" her older self said. "I don't know if you can fix it."

"You have to send us back," Daphne said, her own face wet with tears. "Now that we know what is going to happen, we can change it."

Charming nodded. "My plan exactly, and we're working on a way to do just that. The tears in time pop up all over the place, but by the time I get to one, it has already closed."

"Then we're stuck here?" Sabrina exclaimed.

"No," the future Daphne said. "We may have a way to predict when they come."

Sabrina noticed something unspoken pass between Charming and Daphne's future self. Whatever it was, it made the older Daphne tense.

"People, get back into the house! NOW!" Puck shouted as he pointed toward the sky.

Sabrina looked up and gasped. High in the charcoal sky another dragon sailed overhead. It was green, black, and red, and puffs of smoke drifted out of its wide, reptilian snout. Its roar shook the earth with a boom, and from its gruesome jaws came a torrent of liquid flames that turned a nearby stump into black ash.

The older Sabrina helped Granny wheel her chair into Baba Yaga's house. The rest of the group followed and slammed the door behind them.

"House! Let's move it!" the older Sabrina shouted, and the building once again rose to its feet and raced into the woods.

"Can we outrun that?" Sabrina asked as she watched the dragon blast another nearby tree.

"No," the older Daphne said, rushing to the window and shoving the girls aside. She threw it open and pointed a long thin wand outside. "All we can do is fight. Gimme some water!" she cried. Water blasted out of the wand like it was a firefighter's hose. Unfortunately, the woman's aim was off and it hit the beast in the chest. She cursed herself and shook the wand angrily.

"Not feeling well today, marshmallow?" Puck said. "'Cause if so, I could go out and fight it myself."

"I'm tempted to let you," she replied. "And don't call me that ridiculous nickname."

Daphne stuck her tongue out at her older self. "Hey, cranky. I like my nickname!"

The future Daphne looked at her younger self and a small, almost imperceptible smile crept onto her face. Then she turned back to the open window. "Give me some water."

A torrent of water exploded into the sky like a geyser, and this time it hit the dragon squarely in the mouth. The beast tried to roar, but only a breathy squeak came out. The loss of its most deadly weapon seemed to hinder the dragon's ability to fly as well. It fell to the ground hard and disappeared from view.

"Nice shooting, old me," Daphne said.

"Unfortunately, it's only temporary," Granny Relda said. "Let's hope that we can put some distance between us and it before it reignites its pilot light."

• • •

Sabrina and Daphne were given two cots to sleep in. Without Daphne by her side, Sabrina felt strange and lonely, but most of all concerned that her little sister was feeling the same way. She was about to ask Daphne if she wanted to talk, but a low, rumbling snore came from the little girl. Apparently, the shock of their current situation wasn't causing Daphne any loss of sleep.

"Child," Charming said softly from his cot across the room.

Sabrina sat up and rubbed her eyes. "I'm awake."

"Have you seen Snow?"

Sabrina nodded. "She's worried about you."

Charming nodded as if he shared her feelings.

"I need to know something. How did Daphne get hurt? I mean, the older Daphne. How did she get that scar?"

"It was my fault. I asked her to help me find something. It was dangerous and we ran into trouble," Charming said.

"What kind of trouble?"

"Nottingham."

Sabrina shuddered, imagining the wicked sheriff's serpentine dagger.

"She was helping me recover something," Charming said. "Something that will help us go home. But Nottingham was guarding it, and he . . . well . . ."

Just then, the older Daphne entered the tent. "It appears our little mission has paid off," she said to Charming. "I may have found another tear in time."

"Can you tell us when and where it will be?" Sabrina asked eagerly.

"The Ferryport Landing Cemetery. We need to leave now."

• • •

The adults led the children through the cemetery. There were headstones as far as the eye could see, and a crumbling mausoleum leaning precariously across the path. Weeds had grown over most of the burial plots. None of the cemetery's lamps were working, so the group had to rely on the bluish light of the full moon. It gave everything and everyone a ghostly quality.

"I cannot guarantee the tear will take you back home," the older Daphne said. "In fact, it could put you into an even more dangerous situation."

"What could be more dangerous than running from dragons all day long?" Sabrina said.

"Appearing in the past during the witch trials, for one. Imagine popping up in a Puritan camp and being burned at the stake. Or you could be sent further into the future, when my sister and I are dead and there is no one to protect you from the Scarlet Hand."

"So, we could step through the tear only to find a hungry Tyrannosaurus rex on the other side?" Sabrina asked.

"No, T-rexes weren't native to North America," her older self explained. "But you could step through and find yourself in an ice age thousands of years in the past, or far into the future on the day the sun goes supernova. This isn't a ticket on the Metro-North train. We don't know where you'll end up."

"Then this is too dangerous," Granny Relda said.

"Relda, we know we can't stay here," Charming said. "If there's a chance to get back and make things right, I'll take it. I can't speak for the girls, but I'm going through."

"We'll take our chances too," Daphne said.

Sabrina looked to her sister, surprised by her assertiveness but nodding in agreement. Little chance was better than no chance at all.

"The event should take place within moments," the future Daphne said. "Are you ready?"

Everyone nodded.

"So where is it going to happen?" Charming said impatiently.

The future Daphne took a small black orb out of one of her pockets. It shimmered and soon Daphne was shimmering as well. "Directly above that grave," she said, pointing at a tombstone.

Charming's face blanched. He walked to the grave reluctantly, as if it pained him to stand near it. Sabrina and Daphne joined him, unsure of what had caused the change. Then Sabrina saw the name on the granite headstone: Snow White.

Daphne gasped.

"They killed her," Charming said. "The Scarlet Hand killed her."

"Why?"

Charming shook his head miserably, then grabbed Sabrina and Daphne by the arms. "If we get back, we have to change this. We have to change everything we can."

"We will!" Sabrina said, surprised by his impassioned demand.

Just then, a black cloud covered the sky. It churned like an angry whirlpool, quickly forming a tornado. The abrupt change in the sky was startling.

"That's it!" the older Daphne shouted. "It's coming."

Charming knelt down and caressed the granite as if it were Snow White's delicate face.

"Take care of yourselves, girls," the older Granny Relda said as the cloud got wider and uglier.

"And take care of each other!" the grown-up Sabrina said.

"You too!" Daphne shouted over the wind roaring in their ears.

"Well, Relda! Am I interrupting another tender moment?" a voice said in a loud growl. The group turned to find the Wolf rushing at them. "I hope you don't mind. I brought some friends."

From the horizon Sabrina spotted what appeared to be a small army. They marched toward the group, holding spears, bows and arrows, and swords. On each of their chests was a horrible mark the girls had seen many times: a bloodred handprint. It was the army of the Scarlet Hand.

The future Daphne reached into her overcoat and took out a wand. She turned it on the Wolf and a shock wave came out so powerfully it sent the beast flailing backward over the high trees. Unfortunately, it did nothing to stop the approaching soldiers.

"Sister . . . ," the future Daphne started, but the blond woman was already leaping into action.

"I'm on it," the older Sabrina said. Puck swooped down, scooped her up, and flew her straight toward the approaching soldiers. The two disappeared into the throng, and moments later Sabrina could hear the sounds of clanging swords, groaning men, and Puck's cheers and laughter.

Sabrina heard something zip through the air and saw an arrow land only inches away from her foot. Another arrow whizzed past and hit a nearby tree. She pulled her sister close and looked at Charming and the future Daphne. "I hope this is going to happen soon."

The future Daphne raced to Charming's side and pointed to her face. "Make sure that Nottingham pays for this."

Sabrina looked at the jagged scar on the woman's cheek. She hoped that the rough winds had prevented young Daphne from hearing the terrible conversation.

"I will!" Charming shouted.

Sabrina had a million questions, but she never got a chance to ask them. At that moment the world dissolved right before her eyes.

7

abrina scanned her surroundings. She was lying in the suddenly well-manicured Ferryport Landing Cemetery. The moon was in the sky and her sister and Charming were next to her. She took a deep breath and waited for the sound of an approaching army to break the silence. After a few moments, all she could hear were crickets chirping in the grass. She sat up and took a deep breath, enjoying the clean, crisp air in her lungs. She knew they were home.

Charming sat up and rubbed his eyes. He looked up at the sky then turned and looked behind him. Snow White's gravestone was gone. In fact, the trio was lying in an unused portion of the cemetery.

"I think we're back," Daphne said.

"It appears so," Charming replied. "Though what day it is still presents a problem."

Sabrina smiled and scanned the horizon. She spotted a thin trail of smoke rising into the clouds. "Well, let's go ask someone," she said as she scrambled to her feet. She helped Daphne and Charming up and then marched in the direction of the fire. They walked through the forest until they found an old-fashioned log cabin with a thick stream of smoke drifting out of its chimney. Sabrina's heart froze, convinced that they had returned to the days of the American frontier, but then Charming pointed out the fancy new sports car parked in the driveway.

"We're back where we're supposed to be," he said. "That's the latest model. I had one on reserve before I lost my job."

Charming pounded on the cabin's door, demanding a ride to town, but he only managed to terrorize the homeowner who hid and swore he'd call the police if the filthy man and his "ragamuffin children" didn't get off his property. Sabrina was so angry she could have kicked the prince. If he'd just knocked like a normal person and asked nicely, the three of them might have already been on their way back home. Apparently three months in a doomsday future hadn't stripped Charming of his sense of entitlement.

"Then at least tell me what day it is," Charming demanded.

"I'm calling the cops right now, you lunatic!" the man shouted back.

So they were forced to walk. Sabrina's feet were already killing her from her previous trek into town. As for Charming, he was mostly quiet, though he spent much of the trip attempting to make his tattered clothing and ratty hair presentable.

Several hours later, the trio arrived at Granny Relda's. The house was a very welcome sight, but Charming stopped the girls before they could run inside.

"We should get our story straight," he said.

Sabrina was stunned. "What story? We went into the future. We need to warn everyone about what is going to happen."

"Child, are you really going to go in there and tell everyone you love that they are going to have tragic futures? Your uncle murdered, Canis a savage beast?"

"It is kind of a downer," Daphne said. "But what choice do we have?"

"You have the choice to say nothing," Charming said. "Listen, you have to trust me on this, because I've had a lot longer to think about what I'd do when I got back than you two. The three of us know things. I know exactly how Snow dies. I know who kills her. If I tell her, and word gets out that she knows, I can't prevent the killer from changing his plan. But if I can stop the murderer on the day it occurs, I can stop it from ever happening. You can do the same thing. Do you understand?"

"I don't know," Sabrina said. "We need to tell them. Together we can all work on it."

"Sabrina, it's best if we keep this to ourselves. We can work in the shadows. We can fix things without anyone knowing."

Sabrina looked into Charming's eyes. They were filled with worry, but she could tell he truly believed that sharing what they had seen could lead to bigger problems. Should she trust him? Charming had always been a bit underhanded, and it was no secret that he disliked her family. But he had always been honest.

"Daphne and I can't fix the things that happen to our family on our own," Sabrina said.

"You won't have to," Charming replied. "I'm going to help. Together we're going to fix everything we can, including waking up your parents. I have resources that can help make that happen. I can also give the two of you all the time in the world to find those stolen items. We have to fix everything, girls. Everything! But we can't let anyone get in our way, even if they mean well. Sabrina, you have to trust me."

"I don't know if I can," Sabrina said.

"Then fine! Go in there and tell that fairy boy of yours that you are married to him in the future," Charming said. "Or I can for you if you're so set on sharing."

Sabrina stopped in her tracks and turned to the former mayor. "You wouldn't."

"If we tell, we tell everything," the former mayor said.

She could already feel her face turning red with embarrassment.

Charming laughed. "How does that song go? *Sabrina and Puck, sitting in a tree, k-i-s-s-i-n-g, first comes love—*"

Sabrina watched as her sister started to join the song.

"Shut your traps!" she shouted at both of them. "Fine! We'll do it your way, for now."

Charming nodded. "Very good! It's rare to meet a Grimm that is so reasonable, and I've known quite a number of you."

Just then, the door flew open and Granny and Uncle Jake rushed outside. They huffed across the lawn and wrapped Sabrina and Daphne in bearlike hugs. Elvis followed, knocking Daphne to the ground and covering her in sloppy kisses.

"*Lieblings!* Oh, thank goodness!" their grandmother cried. "We've been looking for you for hours."

The happy reunion didn't last long. Mr. Canis raced across the lawn and snatched Charming off the ground with one of his clawed hands. "If you have touched a hair on their heads, so help me . . ."

"Mr. Canis, he didn't hurt us!" Sabrina shouted. "Put him down."

Canis ignored Sabrina's plea. "Where did you go?"

"We got lost."

Canis scowled. "If you had gotten lost, I would have found you."

"Well, I found them," Charming added as he fought to free himself. "Rather, they found me wandering in the woods, and I helped them get back. Now, put me down, you filthy mongrel."

Canis turned to Granny Relda. The old woman nodded and he set the prince back down on his feet.

"And where have you been?" Granny asked Charming. "You've been missing for three months. My family has torn this town apart looking for you. Snow is out of her mind with worry. You should call her right away."

Charming shook his head. "I wanted to get the girls home safely. I must be going."

"Where?" Sabrina said.

"She's right, pal," Uncle Jake added. "You lost your house when you lost the election. The Queen of Hearts lives there now. Technically you're homeless."

"Oh," Charming said as he stared off at the horizon.

Sabrina couldn't believe what she said next. "You can stay with us."

Granny gasped, but forced a smile. Then she put her hand on Sabrina's forehead. "Are you feeling well?"

"I'm feeling fine, Granny," Sabrina said. If the girls were going to help Charming change the future, it was probably best if he was close by. Sure, he was an arrogant jerk, especially when it came to her family, but she could tolerate a barrage of insults if it would help avert disaster. "Mr. Charming could use some time to get on his feet. He'd do the same for us."

"Don't bet on it," Uncle Jake said.

"Uh . . . Sabrina is right," Granny stammered. "We . . . uh . . . don't have a lot of room, Billy, but you're welcome to it. The sofa is very comfortable."

"What?" Canis growled.

Charming turned to the family. "I couldn't."

"He's right," Mr. Canis said. "He couldn't."

"We insist," Granny said, and she took Charming by the arm and led him into the house.

Canis turned to Sabrina and gave her a look that was both bewildered and betrayed. Sabrina blushed, realizing that she had just invited her friend's bitterest enemy to live with them. He might never forgive her.

"Relda, may I have a word with you?" Canis asked.

Granny turned and approached her oldest friend. "Yes."

"You cannot be serious," Canis said. "He can't be trusted. Don't you recall that he has threatened to destroy this family?"

"I may be old, but my memory is still intact," the old woman said defensively. "Everyone deserves a second chance."

"This man will stab you in the back the first chance he gets. Don't be such a fool!"

"There was a time when people said the same thing about you," Relda said angrily. After a moment she took a deep breath. "Mr. Canis, the decision has been made."

Granny Relda escorted Charming into the house, leaving Canis standing in the yard. He looked angrier than Sabrina had ever seen him, and worse, his anger was directed at her grandmother. Sabrina had never seen Granny Relda and Mr. Canis bicker before, let alone yell at each other. It made her nervous, especially now that she knew the destiny that lay ahead for the old man. Who knew what would make Canis snap and finally surrender to the Wolf? When Canis stomped off into the woods and disappeared, she recalled the secret weapon held under lock and key at the bank. Was it time to retrieve it?

"Nice suggestion, 'Brina," Uncle Jake said as he headed for the house. "You sure you didn't fall and hit your head out in those woods?"

Sabrina and Daphne followed Jake inside, where they found Charming eyeing the couch disdainfully. He turned toward the window and looked outside, as if weighing his alternatives, then turned back and fluffed up one of the couch cushions. "You are very kind. I'll try to stay out of the way."

Puck came down the steps and looked at the girls. "I heard you two were missing," he said to Sabrina.

"We're back," Sabrina replied. She knew her face was bright red. How would she ever forget that she and this smelly, rude, grime-covered boy were destined to be married?

"Darn," he grumbled, then turned and walked back up the steps.

"There goes your future husband," Daphne whispered into her ear.

Yeah, he's a real sweetheart, Sabrina thought.

• • •

Sabrina lay still in her father's old bed. Daphne tossed and turned next to her.

"I'm afraid to go to sleep," the little girl whispered.

Sabrina got out of bed, flipped on the light, and crossed the room to her father's desk. She opened a drawer and took out a hairbrush. Daphne's eyes lit up when she saw it. Brushing Sabrina's hair always seemed to calm Daphne's fears.

"We're back," Sabrina whispered as she sat back down on the bed in front of her sister. "That's what matters. We're back and we can make a difference."

"What if we can't?" Daphne asked as she started to brush her sister's long hair.

Sabrina forced the doubt from her mind. "We have to. The first thing to do is solve the case."

"Do you think Charming can really help us wake up Mom and Dad?" Daphne asked.

"I don't know," Sabrina whispered.

Suddenly, there was a soft tapping at their door. It creaked open and the prince popped his head inside.

"Get dressed and meet me downstairs," he hissed. "We've got work to do."

He closed the door and the girls tiptoed around the room, pulling on jeans and sweaters and shoving their feet into shoes. Then they crept down the stairs, where they found Charming waiting by the door. He had borrowed a pair of Uncle Jake's jeans and a white shirt and had wrapped himself in an old coat, presumably one their late grandfather Basil had owned.

"What's the plan, Stan?" Daphne asked.

Charming gestured for her to be silent and then ushered them outside into the cool spring air. He closed the door tightly, and Sabrina told the house they would be back soon, activating the magical lock. The lock was just one of the protection spells Granny had used on the house.

"I have a few items I need to collect, and I could use the extra hands," Charming said.

"Items? What kind of items?"

"The kind that will change the future," he said. "Unfortunately, they happen to be at the mansion."

Sabrina was shocked. "The mansion! We can't go there. Mayor Heart lives there now. She's got guards!"

"Guards with swords!" Daphne added. "Sharp, pointy swords."

"Yes, I suppose she does," the prince said as if that were a tiny detail.

"Besides, what makes you think she still has these items? From what I hear, she's broken the bank redecorating the mansion. Anything you left behind is probably at the town dump by now."

"Not these things," he said. "If I know Heart like I think I do, she would never throw these out. Oh, here's our ride."

Just then, two headlights pulled into the driveway. When Sabrina's eyes adjusted, she realized she was looking at a long white limousine. The driver's side door opened and a dwarf in a black tuxedo stepped out.

"Good evening, Seven," Charming said.

The dwarf nodded. "Good evening."

"Thank you for taking my call," Charming said, looking down at the ground. He shuffled his feet uncomfortably. In the future, Charming seemed to have respect for Mr. Seven. But in the present, the little man was still Charming's former assistant, and the ex-mayor hadn't been a very nice boss. As Charming's assistant, Seven had been subjected to a steady onslaught of insults and criticisms. Still, the dwarf had been incredibly loyal to the prince, even up to the moment he lost the election and Mr. Seven lost his job. Charming shuffled back and forth as if deciding on whether to apologize for all his abuse. In the end, he simply patted the dwarf on the back.

"Well, as they say in the fairy tales, 'Your chariot awaits,'" Mr. Seven said as if he realized that was as close to an apology as he would ever receive. He rushed to open the door and helped the girls and Charming into the car. Moments later they were pulling away from the house and zipping through the backroads of Ferryport Landing.

"So, what's so important that we have to risk life and limb to sneak into the mansion?" Sabrina asked.

"Amongst other things, a magic detector," Charming said.

"A what?" Daphne asked.

"A device that finds magic," Charming repeated. "Your older self was using it in the future to track the time tears. It is an incredibly powerful magical item. I'm giving it to you tonight."

Daphne smiled. "Thanks!"

"And you think giving it to her is going to change the future?" Sabrina asked.

Charming nodded. "I know it is. See, in the future Daphne and I tracked it down. Giving it to you now alters the time line. It will also allow you to find the devices that were stolen, which obviously never happened in the future."

"Turn the car around," Sabrina said to Mr. Seven. The little man raised his eyebrows in surprise.

"What are you doing?" Charming said.

"I know what happened in the future, when you faced Nottingham," she replied, flashing her eyes toward Daphne. In her mind, she could still see the jagged scar that ran down the future Daphne's face. "I won't let that happen."

"Grimm, neither will I," Charming said, seeming to understand her concern. "I made a promise . . ."

"Absolutely not!"

"Uh, don't I get a say in this?" Daphne said.

"This has nothing to do with you," Sabrina lied.

"You don't have to be a genius to know that I get hurt in the future trying to get this magic detector," the little girl said. "But we have to do this. Solving this case might make a huge difference. I'd rather have a scar than let the world turn out the way it does, or did, or whatever."

"Daphne, I—"

"It's my choice," the little girl interrupted.

"Sabrina, it will make a difference," Charming said, "which is the basis for my plan. I'm going to do everything I can to alter the future by making as many changes as I can now." The prince turned his attention back to his diminutive driver. "What do you know about security?"

"She's got guards at all the doors and windows," Seven said. "Then a few roaming around the house."

"That's not good."

"It gets worse. Nottingham is living in the house. The mayor's a little on the paranoid side and is convinced someone is going to come in and kill her in the night."

"The mayor is smarter than she looks," Charming said. "Good work, Seven. I'm sure the general will give you a medal for this."

"I'm sorry, sir?"

Charming smiled sheepishly, then flipped the switch that raised the divider between the front and backseat.

The limousine snaked its way through the farmlands of the town until it reached the street in front of the mayor's mansion. Seven stopped the car and helped everyone out, then strolled around to the trunk and opened it. Charming scooped up a pile of rope and some flashlights, then closed the trunk.

"This could get dangerous," Charming said to his former assistant.

"Danger is my middle name," Mr. Seven replied as he got back into the car.

"I thought your middle name was Albert," Charming said.

"It is, sir. I was making a joke."

"Oh," Charming said. "Could you stop that?"

Seven nodded.

"Maybe Charming could get a sense of humor," Sabrina whispered to her sister. "That would totally change the future."

Seven started up the limo and pulled into the mansion's driveway. While he drove, Charming led the girls onto the property. They darted from tree to tree, waiting in the shadows as they got closer and closer to the house. It wasn't long before they spotted some of the mayor's guards: men with arms, heads, and legs like people but torsos that were nothing more than extra-large playing cards. Sabrina fought back the dizzy feeling she often got when faced with something that should have been impossible.

Seven parked the limousine by the front door, next to a fountain that had once featured a statue of Charming at its center. Now it contained a marble sculpture of the Queen of Hearts, though substantially thinner and more attractive than the real person. The moment the little man opened the limo door, an obnoxious dance song blasted through the car's brutally loud speakers.

"What's he doing?" Sabrina said.

"Just wait," Charming snapped, as if irritated that she would question the details of his plan.

"Here they come," Daphne said, pointing at a half a dozen of the playing-card guards as they raced to the limo. Shouting over the music, they quickly leveled their swords at Mr. Seven's head. Sabrina couldn't make out what they said, or what he said back, but they seemed to be arguing. A moment later, the front door flew open and Nottingham stormed out, dressed in a robe and slippers, his crooked dagger in his hand.

"Let's go," the prince whispered. He led the girls around the back of the house, where they found a door. Charming tried the handle, but it was locked tight.

"I was hoping this was going to be easy," he said, pulling the rope off his shoulder. One end had a grappling hook attached to it. He tossed it onto the roof and it caught on something. He yanked it hard to test it and gestured to Sabrina.

"You want me to climb this?" Sabrina said.

"Looking at it is not going to get you onto the roof." Charming sneered.

Sabrina shrugged, grabbed onto the rope, and pulled with all her might. She had learned to climb ropes in gym class. The trick wasn't in the shoulders or the arms, it was in the feet. Wrapping the rope around her heels kept her from sliding down and made the whole effort much easier. Soon she was on the roof, looking down at her sister and the prince. Charming had Daphne leap onto his back, and a few anxious moments later, they joined Sabrina.

Charming darted over to the chimney. He peered down into it and felt the bricks. "Good, she hasn't built a fire."

Meanwhile, Sabrina was quickly pulling up the rope. Her heart nearly stopped when one of the guards rushed around the house below her. He ran right by the rope, and though he didn't seem to see it in the darkness, it flicked against the back of his neck. He threw up his hand as if he were shooing a mosquito, and he would have certainly discovered the rope by his ear if Sabrina hadn't been pulling as quickly as she possibly could.

"Bring it over here," Charming whispered.

The girls pulled the heavy rope across the roof the best they could. The prince took it and attached the grappling hook to a rain gutter, giving it a good yank. The gutter creaked but seemed to be stable. Then he tossed the loose end of the rope down into the chimney and hoisted Daphne onto his back.

"We'll go first," he said. "If there happens to be someone waiting for us at the bottom, then climb back down to the lawn and run for your grandmother."

"But you have the rope," Sabrina reminded him.

"Well, then, I guess we're all in deep trouble if there's someone down there."

He climbed into the chimney and Sabrina watched Charming and her sister descend into the darkness below. After several moments, she decided it was her turn. She scaled the chimney side, grabbed the rope tightly, and lowered herself down.

In no time at all her nose and mouth were filled with soot. All the dust made breathing impossible. She leaned against the chimney wall with her back and used her feet to lock herself into place. Then she reached into a coat pocket for a handkerchief, put it up to her nose and mouth, and took shallow breaths until the itching in her throat stopped. Then she shoved the handkerchief back into her pocket and continued on.

Unfortunately, climbing down in the narrow space was extremely difficult. She kept knocking her knees and knuckles against the rough bricks of the chimney. She scraped her back so hard she cried out, and before she knew it, Sabrina hit the floor with a thud. Luckily it wasn't a long drop and she wasn't injured. She looked around to get her bearings and saw the opening of the fireplace before her. If she craned her neck, she could see into the mansion's grand hall. She was just about to crawl out and find Charming and Daphne when she saw two sets of unfamiliar feet.

"What does that moron want?" a woman asked. Sabrina recognized the grating voice. It was Mayor Heart.

"He says that you hired a limousine to take you to a bachelorette party," the second voice said. Sabrina knew that one as well—it was Nottingham, and he was boiling with rage.

"That's nonsense," Mayor Heart cried. "Send him away."

"I'm trying, but the little fool won't listen," Nottingham replied. "I suspect he may be dim in the head."

"Then can't you cut it off and be done with him? I need my rest."

Just then, there was a rush of feet and another man's voice said, "The driver has departed, Sheriff."

"Very good," Nottingham said. "Go back to your post."

"As you wish, sir."

When the man was gone, the wicked duo continued their conversation.

"Nottingham, I'm very distraught over all of this. I doubt that I will ever get to sleep now, unless . . ."

"Don't even think about it!" the sheriff said.

"But my bunions are killing me. Come to my room and rub my feet," Mayor Heart begged.

"Absolutely not!"

"But it's the only thing that puts me to sleep!"

"Try counting tax payments. It eases me to sleep every night."

"DO IT OR I WILL HAVE YOUR HEAD CHOPPED OFF!"

There was a long pause.

"You get fifteen minutes," Nottingham replied. "Not a second more."

"Oh, you're an angel."

Moments later they were gone, and Sabrina crawled out of the fireplace. She scanned the room for Charming and Daphne and spotted them hiding behind a gaudy curtain in the hall. They rushed to her side, struggling to hide their laughter.

"What?" Sabrina whispered angrily.

"You seem to have got a little of the chimney dirt on you when you came down," Charming said.

Sabrina stepped over to a mirror hanging on the wall. In the moonlight she could see she was completely covered in black soot. Her hair, clothes, and every inch of her skin was as black as coal. Worse, she was starting to itch. She gritted her teeth, did her best to regain her dignity, and then turned back to the pair. Neither had a speck of dust on them.

"Naturally," she grumbled. "What now?"

"Follow me," Charming whispered. He led the girls through the rooms on the first floor. He opened each door, took a quick peek inside, and then closed it. Whatever he was looking for was not downstairs, so they were forced to climb the steps. Sabrina, who had snuck out of many places in her life, knew that the best place to walk on stairs was on the edges, as that was where the nails had been placed and so was usually the quietest. She gave the tip to Charming who nodded and did as he was told. Moments later, they had climbed the grand staircase and were exploring the second floor. It wasn't long before they exhausted their search.

"It's in her room," Charming mumbled. "It has to be."

"What's in her room?" Sabrina said.

Charming ignored her question. "We're going to have to go in there."

"What?" Daphne cried. "Nottingham is in there."

Again, Charming ignored them. He walked down a hallway and stopped at a door. Before the girls could argue, he opened it and dragged them through.

Mayor Heart's room was a shrine to herself. There were pictures of her in various gaudy outfits, all of which were covered in little red hearts. Hanging over her bed was a huge ax that Sabrina was sure could easily lop a person's head clean off his shoulders. On the far wall leaned a full-length mirror. Nottingham was slumped in a chair by the mayor's bed. He was sound asleep with Heart's corn-covered foot in his lap, mumbling something about "taxes."

"This way," Charming whispered, walking lightly toward the mirror.

"What are we looking for?" Sabrina grumbled as she watched the sleeping sheriff. She could see his dagger gleaming in the moonlight from the window. A similar sparkle bounced off the ax. She imagined Heart and Nottingham springing from their beds and cutting the intruders to ribbons.

"Nottingham!" the Mayor shouted, and sat up in bed. She was wearing a sleeping mask and was reaching to remove it when Charming snatched the girls and threw them at the mirror's reflection. Sabrina cringed, expecting to smash the glass, but instead she and Daphne flew through it and landed on a marble floor. Charming followed them in and turned back to the portal. He watched as Nottingham reluctantly got out of his chair and checked under the queen's bed and in her closets.

"We're in a magic mirror!" Daphne said as she helped Sabrina get to her feet.

Sabrina was too surprised to respond. She had been in a magic mirror many times, of course. The Hall of Wonders was a breathtaking place, but this magic mirror was simply beyond belief. Instead of a long hallway lined with doors, they were standing in the lobby of a posh hotel. The floors were covered in beautiful Persian rugs. There were plush leather sofas and chairs scattered about and spectacular chandeliers hanging from the ceiling. A wall of windows revealed a beautiful sun-soaked beach just outside with palm trees swaying in the breeze. Sabrina and Daphne approached the windows and gawked at the beautiful scenery. It had been a long time since the sun had shined so brightly in Ferryport Landing.

"Is that real?" Daphne said as she gazed out at the crystal blue ocean.

Charming didn't respond. "Hello?" he said loudly. He stepped up to a long reception desk and leaned over it. "Hello?"

Just then, Sabrina heard a loud bell, and an elevator door opened behind them. A chubby Asian man wearing a Hawaiian shirt stepped out. His face was tanned and his eyes were lined with crow's-feet. A big grin filled the man's face and he hugged Charming.

"Boss! I knew you'd come back to rescue me. Where have you been?"

"I've been out of town, Harry," Charming said, pulling himself away from the man and fussily straightening his clothes. "These are Relda Grimm's granddaughters."

Harry clapped his hands. "Aloha," he said. "Welcome to the Hotel of Wonders. I'm your host, Harry. Checking in?"

"I'm afraid not," Charming said. "I've just come for a few things in my room."

"Right away, sir," Harry said. He raced around the reception desk and opened a drawer containing a collection of old-fashioned hotel keys, each attached to a bright red key chain with a number printed on its front.

"You own a magic mirror?" Sabrina said.

"There is more than one, child," Charming said.

"There is?" Daphne wondered. "Mirror never told us that."

"Found it!" Harry said, as he came around the desk and gestured for the group to follow him. They stepped into an elevator and Harry pushed a button that read PENTHOUSE. The elevator had glass walls, allowing the girls to look out on the beach as they rose into the sky.

"Boss, you have to get me out of here," Harry continued. "Every day Heart gets dressed in front of me. A mirror can only take so much."

"You'll be leaving with us," Charming said.

"Very good, sir. It's good to have you back."

"It's good to be back."

Harry turned to the girls. "So, I heard you mention you have a mirror of your own?"

Sabrina nodded. "Yes, his name is Mirror."

"Hmm, interesting. Odd that he doesn't have a name," Harry replied. "Must have been one of the earlier models."

"Their mirror was originally the Wicked Queen's personal mirror," Charming explained.

"Ah, that explains it. The prototype," Harry said when the elevator stopped and the doors opened.

"I'm confused," Daphne said. "How many magic mirrors are there?"

Harry led them down a hallway decorated with beautiful

paintings. "Oh, that's hard to say! The Wicked Queen made all the magic mirrors. She would create mirrors like this one to fill the particular needs of her customers. She called us the deluxe packages. There are mirrors that are deserted islands, ski resorts, and even one that looks like a Polish restaurant in Cleveland, Ohio."

Charming shrugged. "Everyone has their own taste."

"The prince needed a retreat, a place where he could get away and relax, so naturally the Hotel of Wonders was perfect for him," Harry said proudly. "It's a full-service luxury hotel fit for a prince."

Daphne looked up at Charming. "I always wondered how you stayed so tanned."

"Masters can choose to give their mirrors names. I suppose your Mirror didn't get a name because the Wicked Queen didn't feel it was necessary," Harry explained. "She was never big on personalization. Oh, here we are."

They stopped at a door with a bronze plaque that read THE ROYAL SUITE. Harry inserted the key into the lock and let the group inside. It was a beautiful room with a king-size bed and satin sheets. There was an enormous Jacuzzi and a fireplace in the bathroom, and in an adjoining room a few chairs surrounded an oak bar.

Harry opened two double doors, revealing a walk-in closet filled with expensive suits and shoes, and many drawers and small nooks. Charming selected a long white jacket, which he laid on the bed. Then he picked out a clean black suit, some socks and shoes, and a tie. He lay these on the inside lining of the jacket and they magically sank into it and disappeared.

"Cool! I want one," Daphne said.

Charming nodded. "It's called the Hungry Jacket. It acts like a locker until I want things, then I just reach in and take them."

"It would come in real handy when we get the secret weapon," Daphne said.

Sabrina flashed the little girl an angry look.

"What secret weapon?" the former mayor asked.

Daphne looked around and whistled innocently.

"What secret weapon?"

Sabrina knew there was no use hiding it any longer. "Show him."

Daphne took the necklace out of her shirt and showed Charming the key. "Sheriff Hamstead gave it to us. He said it unlocked a safety-deposit box that held a secret weapon we could use in case Mr. Canis lost control of the Wolf. We're not supposed to get it unless he does, and we're not supposed to tell anyone that we have it."

Charming held the key in his hand for a moment, then gave it back to the girl. "Interesting," he murmured.

"Everything in order, boss?" Harry said. "I had the Cap of Wisdom cleaned, but those rust stains on the Sword of Sharpness are impossible."

"I won't be taking those, Harry," Charming said. He laid some more clothes in the center of the jacket and pulled the four corners together. Then he dropped two of the corners and shook it out. The clothing was gone. "But I'll be needing the magic detector."

Harry nodded and rushed to a drawer across the room. From inside it he removed a small black ball, no bigger than a marble. It was identical to the one Sabrina had seen the future Daphne use. Charming took it from Harry and handed it to Daphne. The little girl marveled at it for a minute. "I feel funny," she said, "like I'm vibrating." And then she did just that. It was disturbing to see the little girl shaking so hard. Sabrina wondered if it hurt.

"You're detecting magic," Charming said. "That should help you find the missing magic items."

"This town is filled with magic items," Sabrina said. "How do we narrow it down?"

"Daphne will feel things of great power automatically,"

Charming explained. "But if she concentrates it will lead her to specific objects. You're going to have to practice. Now, let's go. I've got to get you home before you're missed."

"No time for a break, boss? The spa is offering hot-stone massages," Harry said as he closed the doors of the closet.

"Not today, Harry," Charming replied.

Harry led them out of the room, down the elevator, and into the lobby, where they found the portal that would take them back into the real world. Sabrina looked through it. Nottingham was gone and the mayor was sound asleep.

"I think the coast is clear," she told the others.

"Good luck, folks," Harry said. "It was a pleasure having you here in the hotel. Perhaps you two could come for a longer stay sometime."

Charming flashed Harry a warning look.

"Or maybe not," Harry said. "Well, Aloha and happy surfing."

Charming was the first to step through the portal. Sabrina and Daphne followed, and the sounds of surf immediately disappeared, replaced with Heart's heavy snoring. Charming gestured for the girls to be still, then draped the white jacket over the mirror. When he pulled the garment away, the mirror was gone, just as the clothing had vanished.

"Nice trick," Sabrina whispered.

With the jacket over his arm, Charming crossed the room and carefully opened the door. He craned his neck to look into the hallway and then gestured for the others to follow. Soon they were directly in front of the fireplace.

"I'll go first," Sabrina said, crawling into the fireplace. She searched the space for the rope but couldn't find it. "The rope is gone," she whispered, climbing out quickly.

"Of course it's gone," a voice said from the darkness. The group spun around, but all they could see was a dark figure lurking in the shadows. "I can't just let people break in and out of the mayor's house whenever they want."

Charming clamped his hands on the girls' mouths and pulled them close to him.

"Who are you?" Nottingham asked. A ray of moonlight caught the silver dagger he held in his hand.

Charming moved the girls through the room, careful to stay away from any light that might reveal their identities while also avoiding Nottingham's blade. It wasn't easy. The sheriff was fast and nimble. He lunged forward, slashing the air, and they leaped back.

"Whoever you are, you're either brave or stupid," Nottingham seethed. "Not many would break into the Queen of Hearts's

home. I'll give you credit for being clever, too. Crawling down the chimney was brilliant. I'll have to post a guard on the roof from now on."

Nottingham lunged again. This time Charming threw a punch that caught the sheriff in the face. While he was recovering from the blow, Charming ushered the girls to another part of the room.

Nottingham roared with indignation. Sabrina guessed his pride was hurt more than his face. He leaped at them, swinging his deadly blade in every direction. The girls stumbled backward, avoiding the sheriff the best they could. Unfortunately, the dagger clipped Charming's arm. There was a tearing sound and the prince let out a little groan.

"Aha!" Nottingham cried. He chased Charming around the room, knocking over tables and lamps. Glass crashed to the floor, furniture was overturned, and in the mad, savage assault, the sheriff caught his boot on an upturned rug. He stumbled forward, falling on top of Daphne and knocking her to the ground. Without hesitation, Sabrina leaped on top of him, kicking and punching as she tried to free her little sister. Nottingham, however, seemed undisturbed by Sabrina's attack and held his shiny dagger up to Daphne's face. She cried out, terrified.

"Why, you're just a child," Nottingham said. "Perhaps I should leave you with something to remember me by."

He raised the dagger high over his head, but before its blade could scar Daphne's face, Charming kicked the sheriff in the ribs. The blade flew out of Nottingham's hand and skidded across the floor. As the sheriff clambered to his feet, Charming landed another painful punch to the sheriff's face. Sabrina heard a bone crack, and the villain bellowed in pain, then fell over a chair and hit his head on the floor. After that, he was silent.

"That's for Daphne Grimm," Charming said, standing over the fallen villain, "present and future."

ell, we've already changed a number of things about the future," Charming said when Mr. Seven dropped them off outside of Granny Relda's house. "For one, I have my mirror back and two, Daphne has the magic detector earlier."

"And three, I fought with Nottingham and didn't get a scratch," Daphne said, flashing a smile. "Look at me, I'm still mucho hot-o!"

"I am sorry to have to put you into danger, but—"

"Children, go inside," a voice said from behind them. Sabrina looked up and found Mr. Canis waiting on the porch. "I need to have a word with the prince."

Sabrina could see the anger in the old man's face. "Mr. Canis, we were—"

"Children, go inside," Canis roared.

Sabrina and Daphne started to do as they were told, but the argument began before they were through the door.

"You had no right to take them from the house," Canis said.

"I got them back safely," Charming argued.

"You dare to stand there and be flippant," Canis said. "You snuck them out without permission."

"I did what I had to do, Canis."

"And what exactly was that?"

"I can't tell you."

Canis seethed.

"You're just going to have to trust me," the prince continued.

"Trust you!" Canis said. "Who are you to deserve anyone's trust?"

"That coming from a man who is slowly turning into a killer," Charming bellowed. "Listen, mutt, you want something to trust? Then trust this! I will always work in my own interests, and right now it is in my interest to protect those girls. It is not because I care for them, or have deluded myself into believing that I am part of their family, like you! It's because their well-being serves my current interests."

"Take them from this home one more time and I swear I will kill you," Canis said.

Charming marched up the porch stairs and into the house.

"Do you wish to explain?" Canis asked the girls.

They looked at each other. They had promised not to tell.

"I'm sorry," Daphne said.

"I suspected as much." Canis snapped. He turned and crossed the lawn, disappearing into the woods.

• • •

The next morning, Sabrina woke to the loud thumping of people rushing up and down the steps. She shook her sister awake and pulled her out of bed. When they threw open their door, they found Uncle Jake and Mr. Canis moving furniture out of their grandmother's room and down the stairs.

"What's going on?" she said.

"We've got yet another big day ahead," Granny said as she stepped out of her room. "We're having a yard sale. Get dressed and come down right away. We could use all the hands we can get."

The girls did as they were told and found a crowd gathered on the front lawn, browsing over tables covered with lamps, old books, vases, and assorted knickknacks. All of the items had little price tags on them. Granny sat at a rickety card table with a little gray cash box.

Uncle Jake met the girls on the front porch and together they gazed out at nearly all their possessions. It almost made Sabrina cry to see the old woman selling so many things from her past. "Why is she doing this?"

"We're a little short on the tax bill," her uncle said.

"How short?

"Three hundred thousand dollars," he said.

"Does she really think she's going to make that kind of money at a yard sale?" Sabrina asked.

"Desperate times call for desperate measures," Uncle Jake said.

For most of the morning, people circulated through the tables, haggling over prices and chatting with neighbors. Granny stayed cheery throughout and never seemed insulted when she was told one of her prized possessions wasn't worth what she was asking for it. She rarely turned down an offer, even if it was ridiculously low.

"Relda, tell me about this sword," a golden-haired man said as he studied a blade. Sabrina recognized it immediately. It was a gift from Grandpa Basil and it had hung over her grandmother's bed since the girls had moved in.

"It's a samurai sword from Japan, Sir Kay," Granny explained. "It's Shinto period—a shogun's blade. You can tell from the cherry blossoms carved into the steel. I think it's easily worth ten thousand dollars."

Sir Kay removed the sword from its hilt and examined the blade closely. "How much are you asking for it?"

"I'll take whatever you can offer."

"I'll give you a hundred bucks," Sir Kay said.

Granny sighed. "Sold."

"Granny, no!" Sabrina cried. "You love that sword."

"It's just a sword, Sabrina, and we need the money," Granny replied.

Glinda the Good Witch came over carrying an umbrella stand in the shape of an elephant foot. "You don't happen to be selling anything enchanted, are you, Relda?"

"I'm afraid not," the old woman said.

"Oh well, I'll take this," the witch said, somewhat disappointed. She handed Granny a ten-dollar bill and disappeared into the crowd.

"Mom, you're just giving this stuff away," Uncle Jake complained. He crossed the lawn, waving an old book in the air. "This is a very rare copy of the *Necronomicon*. There's only four or five of these left in existence, and all you want is ten bucks?"

"You and your brother spilled fruit punch on all the pages and then ripped out all the magic spells when you were nine," Granny said. "Its value dropped dramatically."

Uncle Jake frowned and tossed it onto a table, then turned to a crate of old records. "You're selling my Johnny Cash albums? These are worth more than the *Necronomicon*!"

"Granny, if it would help, I could set up a lemonade stand," Daphne offered.

The old woman pulled the little girl close for a hug. "A wonderful idea!"

"Yeah, if we sell each glass for thirty thousand dollars," Sabrina said under her breath. "Where's Charming?"

"He's keeping a low profile," Granny said, gesturing back to the house.

Sabrina spotted him peering through the curtains. She nudged her sister so she could see the prince as well.

Just then, a police car pulled up and parked along the road. Nottingham stepped out of it and approached the yard. Sabrina could see he had a white bandage over his nose, and two black eyes.

"Hello, Sheriff," Granny said, trying to sound chipper.

"Selling your trash, are you, Grimm?" the sheriff sneered. "I doubt you could give away most of this."

"Well, you know what they say, one person's trash is another person's treasure," the old woman replied.

Nottingham laughed. "You know what else they say? There's a

sucker born every minute." He picked up an African mask Sabrina had seen in her grandmother's bedroom, flipped it over, and dropped it back to the table as if it were a wad of used tissue.

"Seems as if you've had an accident," Granny said.

Nottingham's lip curled. "Yes . . . an accident."

"You need to be more careful," Granny said.

"Thank you for your heartfelt advice," Nottingham seethed. "By the way, you wouldn't be selling any full-length mirrors this afternoon, would you?"

Granny smiled and shook her head. "Not today. Perhaps you'd be interested in a paperweight or a pair of sunglasses! No one would see your eyes."

Nottingham sneered. "Perhaps I should buy a chair. It might be fun to watch your desperate little play. Though I know how it's going to end—in foreclosure."

Uncle Jake brought over a high-backed chair and set it down. "This one is twenty bucks."

Nottingham laughed. He paid Granny Relda and sat down. "Money well spent," he sang.

He was grinning like it was his birthday when former deputies Boarman and Swineheart arrived. They were two of the Three Little Pigs, former police officers and good friends of the Grimms.

"Hello!" Granny said. "Can I interest you in anything? We've got some great bargains here."

Boarman and Swineheart nodded and snorted at Nottingham. "How much money have you raised so far, Relda?" Swineheart asked.

"Oh, I think we've gotten a thousand dollars so far," the old woman said sheepishly.

Sabrina cringed. The sale had been going on for four hours and they weren't even close to raising the full three-hundred-thousand-dollar tax bill.

Boarman picked up a letter opener. It had a marble handle and roses engraved in the steel. "This is beautiful," the portly man said.

"Yes, my husband bought that for me when we made a stop in Paris," Granny said wistfully.

"I'll take it," Boarman said. He reached into his pocket and took out an enormous roll of money, then handed it to Granny Relda.

"Mr. Boarman, you've given me too much. The letter opener is only ten dollars," the old woman said.

Boarman smiled and shook his head. "I think you're wrong. The price tag says ten thousand dollars."

Sabrina was stunned silent, as was nearly everyone else. Everyone but Nottingham, that is. The man was so shocked, he nearly fell out of his chair.

When it was Swineheart's turn, he selected a set of silver steak knives in an oak box. "I'll take these," he said, tossing an even bigger wad of cash on the table. Sabrina noticed the price tag said twenty-five dollars. She guessed Swineheart had paid as much as twenty-five thousand.

"Gentlemen!" Granny said. "This is much too generous."

"What is the meaning of this?" Nottingham cried.

That's when Briar Rose appeared. Behind her was a group of Everafters the family had known for years: Mr. Seven, King Arthur, Geppetto . . . the line went on and on. Each was carrying a huge stack of money.

"You've been good friends to us," Briar said, then turned to Uncle Jake. "And I can't exactly date a guy who's homeless."

"But this is outrageous," Granny said. "I can't accept this money. You're giving away a small fortune."

"No worries," Mr. Seven said as he approached the table. "We live in Ferryport Landing. What are we going to spend our money on anyway?"

The crowd bought every little knickknack they could for ridiculous sums of money. With each sale, Nottingham seemed to have a new apoplectic fit. He fumed and raged and threatened, but the sales went on.

As the girls watched from the porch, they heard a tapping behind them and realized Prince Charming was trying to get their attention. They went inside to meet with him.

"What are you doing? Why aren't you working on the case?" he demanded.

"We're stuck helping out with the yard sale," Sabrina answered. "You know, we're only kids. It's not like we can just hop in a car and drive downtown."

"Not again, at least," Daphne said, reminding her sister of the time they had taken the car for a spin.

"Well, haven't you ever snuck out before? This is the perfect opportunity. Your grandmother is distracted. Take the magic detector and go! If she asks for you, I'll tell her you're upstairs fussing with your hair or playing dolls."

"Is that what you think we do with our free time?" Sabrina said, aghast.

"Just go!"

The girls raced up stairs to retrieve the magic detector and nearly knocked over Puck in the hallway.

"What are you doing hiding up here?" Sabrina asked.

"There's hard work going on outside and, as you know, I'm allergic," he said. "I once carried a box for the old woman and nearly had to be hospitalized. Why aren't you two helping?"

"Uh . . . we're just going to our room," Sabrina stammered.

"Do you smell that?" Puck asked.

"Smell what?" Daphne said.

"A lie. I smell a lie and it's stinky. What are you two up to?"

Sabrina knew the fairy would never give up, so she dragged him into her bedroom with her sister in tow. "We're investigating the stolen magical items on our own," Sabrina said.

"And you don't want the old lady or Canis to find out? That's incredibly sneaky and dishonest."

The girls nodded with shame.

"I'm in," Puck said. "We can crawl out of your bedroom window and I'll fly you wherever you want."

"You want to change your pants, first," Daphne said.

Puck glanced down at his filthy jeans. "No. Why?"

"They don't fit you anymore."

Sabrina studied the boy's pants. Normally the cuffs dragged on the ground and into whatever Puck stomped through, but now they were several inches above his ankles.

"They must have shrunk in the wash," Puck said.

"Since when do you wash your clothes?"

Puck shrugged. "Are we going to do this or not?"

Daphne grabbed the little black ball that detected magic from the bureau and slipped it into her pocket. Then she joined Sabrina and Puck at the window. They opened it and Puck leaped out. A second later his wings were flapping and he was hovering outside. He reached out his hand for Sabrina's. She eyed it as if it were something she didn't understand, like algebra or diagramming sentences. She snatched it quickly before the boy threw a fit, though she caught her sister's grin out of the corner of her eye. Before she had seen their future together, Sabrina wouldn't have thought twice about holding the boy's hand, except to remember to wash later with generous amounts of antibacterial soap and a wire brush. But now even something so simple seemed to have so many complicated layers to it.

"Don't you say a word," Sabrina grumbled to her sister.

In no time, the trio was sailing above the treetops out of sight of their family and friends on the front lawn. Once they were over Main Street, Daphne began to shimmer and vibrate.

"I'm picking up something," she said.

"Remember what Charming said," Sabrina replied. "Concentrate on what we're looking for. Think about the clock and the wand and the water."

Daphne agreed and closed her eyes tightly. "I can't explain why, but I feel like we should head toward the river."

Puck dropped them off out of sight of the human townspeople, which was harder than it sounded. The streets were quite crowded with people trying to sell their jewelry and watches. It was Friday—the last day to pay the taxes. People were desperate.

The children walked down the road as Daphne described the sensation she got from the magic detector. As they continued, the feeling got stronger, which was good, but Daphne was visibly, violently shaking, which was bad. Sabrina was sure someone would notice eventually. They walked down to the end of the street, where Ms. Rose's coffee shop, the radio station, and a few other businesses sat. There the vibration was stronger than ever.

"Are you OK?" Puck asked as he watched the little girl turn into a blur.

"I feel funky," Daphne said. Her voice sounded like she was talking through an electric fan. "I have a feeling we're really close. It's hard to pinpoint exactly where they are, though. I think I need more practice."

Suddenly, the vibrations stopped. "I need a break," the little girl continued. "I think I might ralph."

They stopped outside of Sacred Grounds and spotted Briar Rose through the window. She was sitting with several women, showing them the coffee mug she had purchased at Granny's yard sale. Next to her at the table were Ms. White, Dr. Cindy, and another woman with long, flowing red hair whom the girls had never seen before. They were all trying to console Ms. White, who was in tears.

"Charming is a jerk," Daphne said as she looked through the window. "He's broken her heart. He should at least call her."

"I think he's trying to protect her," Sabrina said.

"Let's go in and try to cheer her up."

"We're wasting time," Sabrina said. "We need to keep looking for the stolen items."

"I don't care," Daphne declared. "Ms. White is my friend."

"Fine with me," Puck chimed in. "I'm starving. I'm getting in line for a muffin."

The children entered the coffee shop, and the girls crossed the room to greet the four women.

"Hello!" Daphne said, grinning from ear to ear.

"Hello, girls," Briar Rose replied. "Taking a break from the big sale?"

The girls nodded.

"What's wrong, Ms. White?" Daphne asked.

"Snow is having a difficult day," Cindy said.

"I'm just worried about Billy," the teacher said with a sniffle.

Sabrina and Daphne shared a look.

"I'm sure he's fine," Sabrina said.

"That's what I've been telling her," the fourth woman said. Her red hair framed her creamy complexion and green eyes. To Sabrina she looked like a glamorous star from an old black-and-white movie. She reached over and shook Sabrina's hand. "You must be Henry's girls. I'm Rapunzel."

Daphne let out a squeal.

"She does that for everyone?" Cindy asked with a laugh. "I thought I was special."

"We're trying to cheer up Snow," Rapunzel said. "William doesn't deserve your tears, girlfriend."

"She's right, Snow," Briar Rose said. "Whenever his pride is hurt, he runs off—hunting, he used to call it, but I knew better. He was sulking. Losing the election hurt his fragile ego."

"And William does have his childish moments," Cindy added. "I was married to the man for nearly a hundred years. He'd throw his tantrums, disappear, and then show up without any explanation. He'll be back."

"But I can't believe he wouldn't call, write, leave me some way of knowing he was OK," Ms. White sobbed.

Rapunzel sighed. "You thought you were different."

Snow wiped her eyes. "What?"

"You thought you were different from us," the red-haired beauty repeated. "You thought that because you two had found one another after five hundred years that your love was special. I thought the same thing. All the magic that surrounded my love affair with William, both emotionally and literally . . . I mean, that's why they call our stories fairy tales, right—love and magic and riding off into the sunset together?"

"Rapunzel, you've got this all wrong," Ms. White replied. "I didn't think I was special."

"The thing is . . ." Cindy said, "you *are* special."

Rapunzel and Briar Rose shifted uncomfortably.

"I knew it. We all knew it," Cindy continued. "We're all amazing women: beautiful, smart, capable. But we weren't Snow White."

"Cindy—"

But the blond beauty stopped Ms. White. "This isn't out of anger, Snow. I'm over that. But I'm a person that understands relationships. I had a family that was completely nuts, and I was married to a guy who was more boy than man. I know the truth when it's looking me in the face. He never got over you, and that's why I left him. William has always loved you. Not that he didn't love Briar, or Rapunzel, or me. I believe he tried to be a good husband to each of us. But his heart was always yours. You were the first woman in his life, and when you left him at the altar, he never recovered."

"We were too young. It was all happening so fast," Ms. White explained.

"I wish I had been that smart," Rapunzel said. Briar Rose nodded in agreement.

Cindy reached over and took Ms. White's hand. "For a long time I resented you, Snow, because I was always competing with you. Your spirit hung over our home like a ghost. Occasionally, we would be at a party and hear about something that was going on in your life and his eyes would fix on whoever was saying it. For days he would be distant, distracted. He'd spend a week at the stables, claiming the horses needed attention, but I wasn't stupid."

"Is this true?" Ms. White said, looking at the other women in the group. They all nodded. "I'm sorry."

"Snow, I don't think Cindy is chastising you," Rapunzel said.

"No, in fact, Snow, since I've come to know you I adore you, and I don't regret anything—my Tom is all the prince I will ever need. What I'm trying to say to you is that William's love for you is different. It *is* troubling that he hasn't tried to contact you."

"There goes Dr. Cindy," Rapunzel said. "Could you turn off the honesty you give your callers and remember we're trying to cheer this woman up?"

Snow White laughed and the others joined her.

"Ms. White, I know he loves you," Daphne said. "He's going to pop up any day now."

"I hope you're right," Ms. White said.

"Well, when he does, I hope you give him a karate kick to the behind," Briar Rose said, which caused the four women to burst into laughter again.

"Briar, I swear, you don't say much, but when you do it's hilarious," Rapunzel said. "Girls, I've got an idea, and you can tell me I'm nuts and say forget it, but how about we make this a regular thing?"

The women glanced at one another hesitantly.

"Come on!" Rapunzel cried. "We've been avoiding each other in this silly little town for two hundred years! Let's put it all behind us, meet for brunch, start a book club, gossip. Let's be friends!"

"I don't know," Cindy said hesitantly.

"What if we played poker?" Briar Rose suggested.

"I'm in," Ms. White said quickly.

Dr. Cindy threw up her arms in surrender. "How are Tuesday nights?"

"Can I come?" Daphne asked.

The table roared with laughter. "Of course you can come," Ms. White said.

"So that settles it," Rapunzel replied. "Tuesday nights at my place. You bring the wine and I'll make something decadent that we shouldn't eat. We'll call ourselves the Poker Princesses."

The women nodded enthusiastically, and even Sabrina joined in.

Puck came over with a sack of muffins. "What's all the commotion?"

"And no boys!" Rapunzel cried, and the Poker Princesses applauded.

Puck grumbled and stormed out of the coffee shop. Sabrina grabbed her sister, said their good-byes, and chased after the fairy.

"We've got to get back," Sabrina said as they left. "Granny is going to miss us."

• • •

Oddly, Granny hadn't missed them. There had been a run at the yard sale and nearly three quarters of the items were sold. When the children landed in the backyard and circled the house to check in with the sale, they found their grandmother counting a huge stack of bills. Puck rushed up to his room for fear of being drafted into helping put things away.

"Oh, hello girls," Granny said. "As they say in the business world, we made a killing."

"Enough to pay the taxes?" Daphne asked.

Granny Relda nodded. "Enough to put us over the top, I think. If you'll help Mr. Canis bring what's left back into the house, we can go down and pay the bill. It will be nice to have this off my shoulders."

The children carried the rest of the things back inside and put them in their original places. When everything was settled, the house seemed emptier. Paintings were gone, as was the overstuffed chair in the living room. Most of the rugs and kitchen utensils had been sold, including the toaster and the coffeepot. Daphne was heartbroken when she discovered Granny had sold the ice-cream scoop.

Suddenly, Charming's full-length mirror, which he had leaned on the wall of the living room, began to warp and shimmer. The prince stepped through the reflection and into the room. He sported a fresh shave and haircut, and he had swapped Uncle Jake's jeans for a stylish, clean suit. Apparently, the Hotel of Wonders lived up to its reputation as a full-service resort.

"Swanky," Daphne said.

"Perhaps later you'll give me a tour of your mirror," Granny Relda said. "I've never been inside any but our own."

Charming nodded. "Perhaps."

"Well, I suppose I should go and fetch Mr. Canis and Jacob,"

Granny said as she hurried upstairs. "We've got the tax money. Oh, I do so hope that it ruins Mayor Heart's day."

When she was gone, the children turned to Charming.

"What did you find?" he asked.

"Whoever has the stolen items has got them stashed somewhere near the river. We were picking up big vibes down by Sacred Grounds and the radio station."

"Mucho huge-o vibes," Daphne added, and then her tone turned angry. "We also saw Ms. White."

"How is she?" Charming asked.

"Heartbroken!"

Charming lowered his eyes.

"She's a mess," Sabrina said. "You should send her a note, anything, just to let her know you are OK. She thinks you're dead."

"I can't," he said.

"But—"

"Stop! My decision is final," Charming shouted. "I know you don't understand. I can't expect you to. It's not easy to know she is hurt and that it is my fault, but you should know that I would do anything for her—anything!"

"Fine," Sabrina said, throwing her hands up. Daphne frowned but didn't argue.

Granny returned with Mr. Canis and Uncle Jake. The old man looked at Charming with distaste.

"Girls, how would you like to see the mayor's head pop off?" Granny asked. "Want to come with us to the tax office?"

"I wouldn't miss that for the world." Sabrina smiled.

Uncle Jake reached into his pocket and took out a camera. "I'm taking pictures!"

"William, since you are in hiding, would you mind looking after the house while we're gone?" the old woman asked.

"Do you think it is wise to leave him here alone?" Canis demanded before Charming could answer.

Granny flushed. "Mr. Canis!"

"You think I'm going to rob you blind?" Charming asked.

"I think you might try," Canis said, hovering close to Charming's face.

"Gentlemen! That's enough!" Granny shouted.

Canis nodded reluctantly and stormed outside. Sabrina could hear him slam the car door, and then the family's ancient car engine roared to life, spitting and knocking violently.

When everyone got into the car, Canis threw the old jalopy into reverse and whipped out into the street. When he put it into drive, the engine screamed like a cat in a bathtub. Canis ignored its protests and pounded his foot onto the accelerator.

"That was entirely uncalled for!" Granny shouted over the noise.

"Having him in the house is entirely uncalled for!" Canis yelled back.

Sabrina and Daphne were shocked. Even when they'd fought the last few days, the girls had never heard Mr. Canis raise his voice at their grandmother. In a world filled with people the old man couldn't stand, Granny Relda had always had his utmost respect.

"I know that the two of you have had your history," Granny said. "But the man is homeless."

"That man deserves no better than to be homeless."

"It is not in my habit to turn away a person in need," Granny said.

"Then you are a fool!" Canis declared.

"Was I a fool when I took you in?" Granny shouted back. "When even my husband told me you were untrustworthy, I turned a deaf ear. And you have become the dearest friend I have and my most trusted companion."

Canis was silent but steaming.

"I'm sorry about the angry words," Granny said when the family finally reached the courthouse. "Let's try to forget them. Today is a happy day."

Canis grunted and looked out of the window. "I'll wait here."

The crowd of protesters from the day before was gone. Only a few stragglers remained, and they looked even more desperate. This time they showed no resistance to letting the family pass. Granny, Uncle Jake, and the girls climbed the steps and went inside. The security guard they had met the day before was standing in the same spot. He seemed surprised to see the family. They waved to him and continued down the hallway to the tax office. Once inside, Granny rang the bell for service.

"I really can't wait to see her face," Granny said softly.

It wasn't long before Mayor Heart came around the corner. She spotted the family and gasped. "What are you doing here?"

"We've come to pay our taxes, of course," Granny said, setting a bag of money on the countertop.

The woman snatched her megaphone and raised it to her crooked mouth. "THAT'S NOT POSSIBLE! NOTTING-HAM!" she shouted, then slammed the device down on the countertop so hard Sabrina thought it might break.

"Someone's having a bad day," Daphne said with a grin.

Seconds later, Sheriff Nottingham hobbled into the room. "What is it, woman? Don't you know I have my hands full? The phone is ringing off the hook. Apparently some fool in a civil war uniform is over on Applebee's farm firing a musket!"

"The Grimms have come to pay their taxes . . . AGAIN!" Heart said, pointing an angry finger at the family.

The sheriff nodded, but his face was dark and angry. "I know."

"It's all there, Sheriff, and like before I'm going to need a receipt," Granny Relda said.

"You're enjoying this!" Heart shouted.

"What? Paying taxes? I doubt there are too many people who enjoy it," Granny said.

"Well, you can come in here with a million dollars next time and it won't change the inevitable. I want you out of this town, Relda Grimm—you and your filthy brood. I want every human being out of Ferryport Landing, and what I want I get."

Suddenly, the door flew open and one of the playing-card soldiers raced inside.

"Sheriff, we've got a situation!" he yelled.

"Calm yourself down, you idiot!"

"There's a ship coming up the river," the solider said. "I just heard about it on my radio. The witnesses say it's pretty old."

"So what," Nottingham said. "Ships come up and down the river every day."

"This one has cannons mounted on it," the guard said.

"Cannons?" Granny repeated.

Just then, the walkie-talkie strapped to the guard's waist squawked and a voice came on. "Seven of Clubs, you're not going to believe this ship. There must be a thousand people on it, and they're all dressed like they're going to a costume party. Plus, you gotta see this storm. It just came out of nowhere. Wait a minute . . . I think the boat has a name painted on the side. It looks German . . . '*Neuer Anfang*.'"

"New Beginning," Granny translated.

"It can't be!" Mayor Heart shouted.

Nottingham leaped over the counter that divided the room and pushed through the family as he raced out the door. Mayor Heart was hot on his heels.

"What?" Sabrina cried. "What's the big deal about this ship?

Uncle Jake shook her head in disbelief. "It's impossible. It can't be the *New Beginning*."

Mr. Canis was already out of the car and hurrying to join them when they exited the courthouse. "You've heard?"

Granny nodded. "It must be some kind of prank."

"It's not," Canis said. "I can smell the boat. I'll never forget that smell."

The family raced down the street as fast as they could. By the time they reached the tiny marina, Granny Relda was out of breath and there was a huge crowd of people looking out on the

river. The Grimms weaved through the mob until they got to the front. There it was: a massive sailing ship with several white flags fluttering in the cool spring breeze. Even from the shore Sabrina could see a crowd on board staring back at them. A tiny rowboat was already cruising toward the shore with a lone man at the oars.

"Who is it?" Daphne wondered, looking across the river.

Granny reached into her huge handbag and took out a pair of binoculars. "Oh dear," she said when she peered through the lenses.

"What? Who is it?" Sabrina asked, and Granny handed her the binoculars. She adjusted them and looked out toward the ship. The deck was filled with princes, princesses, witches, ogres, dwarves, oddly dressed people, and numerous hairy and feathered creatures. She searched the water for the rowboat. A man with brown hair and a rather large nose was approaching the shore. He seemed oddly familiar, as if she had seen a picture of him before, or maybe a drawing . . . Then it dawned on her who it was.

"Children, that's your great-great-great-great-great-grandfather. That's Wilhelm Grimm," Granny said.

9

abrina glanced at the sky. A swirling black storm—
another tear in time—was rapidly vanishing from
above the river.

The little rowboat drifted to the shore and Wilhelm leaped
out. He was shorter than Sabrina expected. He was wearing a
long brown coat and a wide-brimmed hat. His eyes were almost
black and quite small. He turned and gazed at the crowd with
awe and wonder.

"Ist das Amerika?" Wilhelm asked.

"Ja, das ist Amerika. Willkommen, Wilhelm. Willkommen,"
Granny said.

"What did you just say?" Daphne asked.

"I just welcomed him to America," Granny said, then turned
back to Wilhelm. "Do you speak English?"

"*Ja*, a little," Wilhelm said. "Is this New York?"

Granny nodded.

Wilhelm studied the crowd. He spotted Briar Rose on the shore and rushed to her. Confused and excited, he took her hand, then looked back at his ship. *"Wie sind Sie hier herkommen? Waren Sie auf dem Schiff?"* he asked.

"What is he saying?" Ms. Rose asked.

"He's confused," Granny explained.

"How can you be here?" Wilhelm turned and pointed at the ship. "And there?"

Before anyone could explain, Nottingham pulled handcuffs from his jacket and clamped them around Wilhelm's wrists. "Ask him if he understands he's under arrest."

Nottingham led Wilhelm from the marina toward the town jail. Granny was at the head of a crowd demanding the man's release, while also doing her best to explain what was happening to the family's bewildered ancestor.

As she left, Granny instructed Sabrina and Daphne to stay with Mr. Canis and to help make sure that no one else rowed from the *New Beginning* to shore or from the marina to the ship.

"I'm on that boat," Briar Rose said as Uncle Jake took her hand. "I mean, I was on that boat. I mean . . . I don't know what I mean."

"How did this happen?" Mr. Seven asked, pushing his way through the crowd.

Sabrina and Daphne looked at each other. They knew exactly how it happened. They just didn't know who or what was causing it. Apparently, their conspiratorial look wasn't lost on Mr. Canis. He snatched them both by the arm and dragged them out of earshot of the crowd.

"You know something," he said.

Sabrina did her best to play innocent. She glanced over at Daphne, who was whipping her head around, trying to avoid the old man's eyes.

"I don't know what you're talking about," Sabrina mumbled.

"Child, this is no time for lies," Canis growled.

"We promised Mr. Charming that we wouldn't say anything," Daphne blurted out. Sabrina scowled. Daphne was just no good at lying.

Canis bristled. "I should have known he had something to do with this."

"You've got it wrong, Mr. Canis," Sabrina said, throwing her hands up in surrender. "He's trying to help."

"Help who?"

"It's going to sound crazy."

"Try me," the hulking man said. Sabrina looked up into his

face. She saw his wolfen features, clearer every day, and realized he might actually understand. "It's a tear in time," Sabrina said. "It's been happening all over town, but this is the biggest incident yet."

"A tear in what?"

"In time. Things are slipping out of the future and the past."

"And how do you know this?"

"Because we slipped through one ourselves," Daphne said. "Yesterday when you took us out into the forest we didn't get lost. We got sent to the future!"

"We went fifteen years ahead," Sabrina added.

"How does Charming have anything to do with this?" Canis asked impatiently.

"He was stuck there too. He'd been pulled into one of these tears right after the election," Daphne said. "He had been trying to find a way back for months."

"Why didn't you tell anyone?" Canis asked.

"Charming made us promise to keep it to ourselves. We know things . . . about the future. He thinks that we should keep them a secret so we can change things without anyone getting in the way."

"What is so bad about the future that needs to be changed?" Canis asked.

A tear rolled down Daphne's cheek. "You weren't in the future. The Wolf was."

Canis looked shaken but controlled himself.

"We're trying to change as much as we can," Sabrina said. "You can't tell anyone, not even Granny."

"How do we stop these time tears?" Canis asked.

"We don't know," Daphne said. "We've got something that helps us find them, but I'm not very good at using it yet."

"We think that all those stolen magical items we've been investigating are being used together, and they're causing the tears," Sabrina explained as best she could. "We know that in the future we never found the missing items. If we can locate them, we might be able fix the tears and change the future at the same time."

Just then, an enormous fiery explosion smacked into the beach, sending rock and sand in all directions. When Sabrina searched for the source of the attack she noticed that one of the cannons on the ship had smoke coming out of it.

"They're firing on us!" Sabrina exclaimed.

"Of course, we just arrested their captain," Canis said, rushing back to the dock. "Those aren't pebbles they're throwing at you, people. Get back!"

Another blast rocked the beach.

"Are we going to stand here and let them fire on us?" King Arthur shouted as he stepped through the crowd. "Shouldn't we fire back?"

"Not if you don't want to wipe out your own existence," a saggy-jowled man said from the crowd. Sabrina thought at first that he was just an old man, but then she realized his wrinkled skin wasn't skin at all but an old burlap sack. He had straw sticking out of his cuffs, and he wore an old farmer's hat on his head.

"What are you talking about, Scarecrow?" Mr. Seven shouted.

"That ship has clearly sailed here from the past. How and why, I can't say, but I do know one thing: Many of us are on that ship. Arthur, you're on that boat, but it's you from two hundred years ago. If you attack that ship, you could accidentally kill yourself."

"Scarecrow, I never can make heads or tails of anything you say," one of the Three Blind Mice complained. "You sure the Wizard gave you brains? I got a feeling he stuffed your head with cotton candy."

"Oh, if you only had a brain," the Scarecrow replied.

Canis stared at the Scarecrow. "So, are you saying that if someone from that ship was killed, it could change the present?"

The Scarecrow nodded. "Absolutely."

In a flash, Canis had the girls in his arms and was running up the street. "What are you doing?" Sabrina yelled.

"Nottingham's got Wilhelm!" he shouted. "If he knows what the Scarecrow knows, he will kill him."

"Why would he do that?" Sabrina asked.

"Because if Wilhelm were to die, then the barrier that traps us in this town would never have been created," Canis said. "And killing him would put an end to his descendants. Every member of your family could suddenly cease to exist."

"Fudge," Daphne whispered.

Sabrina looked back at the crowd by the river. As she watched, many of the bystanders started chasing after them. It seemed that they had realized the dark opportunity Canis had just explained. "Uh, could you run a little faster?" she said.

The jailhouse was a mob scene. There were hundreds of Everafters outside, demanding answers. Canis set the girls on his huge shoulders and tossed people aside as he pushed his way into the tiny building. They found Granny at the front desk, pounding on the table and calling out for the sheriff.

"Where is he?" Canis said, setting the girls down.

"Nottingham has taken him back to a cell for interrogation," she said.

"I worry about how he defines the word 'interrogation,'" Canis said. "We have to get him out of there."

Granny nodded.

Then the sheriff stepped back into the office. He had a grin on his face like he had just gotten a bicycle for his birthday.

"Sheriff Nottingham!" Granny exclaimed. "You had no right to arrest that man."

"I have every right. I'm the sheriff," he said.

"What is his crime?"

"Let's see. He doesn't have a sailing license, or a passport, and he's trying to sneak foreigners into the country."

"He doesn't belong here, Nottingham," Canis said. Sabrina and Daphne both tugged on his sleeves, hoping to remind him that it wasn't wise to tell what he knew about the time tears.

"Oh, I'm well aware he doesn't belong here," Nottingham said. "He's come here from the past. Now that I see it with my own eyes, I almost feel like apologizing for ignoring all the reports I've been getting from citizens. The phone has been ringing off the hook for days about the Lenni Lenape Indian tribe, dinosaurs, Civil War soldiers, spacemen . . . Still, none of them really deserved my attention until today. It seems as if the past has opened up and delivered us a gift."

"Gift! What are you talking about?" Granny demanded.

"Why, with one slash of my dagger, I can end the suffering of this entire town," Nottingham replied. "If I am not mistaken, the man back in that cell is Wilhelm Grimm. Killing him gives us our freedom."

"You can't just kill a man," Sabrina said. "You're a police officer."

"Police officer?" Nottingham laughed. "Child, do you think I took this job because I care about justice? Your precious Wilhelm is being put to death for crimes against Everafters. If my theory is correct, when he expires, your wretched family will vanish just like that!" He snapped his fingers so loudly that Daphne jumped in fright. "I wonder if I'll remember you when it's all said and done. It would be a shame if I didn't."

"When do you plan to do this?" Granny Relda asked.

"Midnight tonight!" a voice shouted through a megaphone. The crowd separated and Mayor Heart stepped front and center. "Tonight I make good on my campaign promise of changing everything. I bet you didn't guess just how much change I had planned. It's going to be quite a celebration, folks. Everyone is invited."

Nottingham let out a wicked laugh as he glared at the Grimm family. "Aren't you going to tell us we'll never get away with this?"

The crowd roared with laughter.

"I thought it was understood," Granny Relda said calmly.

The family pushed their way through the mob and out into

the street. Uncle Jake was waiting by the car when they arrived.

"Is he in there?" he asked, pointing back toward the jail.

Granny nodded. "Heaven only knows how he got here."

Sabrina and Daphne shared a look but kept quiet.

"What are we going to do?" Sabrina asked.

"Yeah, I don't want to not exist. I've got plans," Daphne added.

"We're going to do what every Grimm has done in times of trouble. We're going to work together as a family. Mr. Canis, take us home. We have to rally the troops."

• • •

"You want to *what*?" Uncle Jake said, leaping from his seat on the family couch.

"I want you to tell Baba Yaga that Nottingham has her wand and lead her to the police station," Granny said.

Charming, Canis, Sabrina, Daphne, Puck, and even Elvis seemed shocked by Granny's plan. They gazed at one another in disbelief.

"What in heaven for?" Uncle Jake asked.

"We're going to need her as a distraction," the old woman explained. "If she can cause enough of a ruckus, Nottingham won't hear Mr. Canis knocking down the back wall so we can break Wilhelm out of his cell."

Puck clapped his hands. "A jailbreak. I love it!"

Uncle Jake, however, stood shaking his head. "Mom, mutual trust is the only thing keeping Baba Yaga from adding all of us to her bone fence. If you lie to her, things will get ugly."

"Things are ugly," Mr. Canis said. "Desperate times, son."

"I know the consequences," the old woman said, "but the alternative is much worse."

"Personally, I think your job sounds a lot more fun than mine," Puck complained to Uncle Jake.

"I'm sorry you feel that way, Puck," Granny said. "But your task is the most important."

"What about us?" Daphne said as she rubbed Elvis's chin. The big dog watched Granny Relda attentively as if waiting to find out what his role in the plan would be.

"You girls are going to stay with me. I may need your help getting Wilhelm to safety," Granny said.

"But there's a hole in your plan, general," Charming said.

"'General'?" Granny Relda said.

The girls and Charming shared a look.

"I mean . . . what are you going to do with Wilhelm when you get him? You won't be able to hide him here. Nottingham is going to know who was responsible."

Granny shook her head. "I don't know. All I do know is that if we don't rescue him, the queen is going to kill him and then my family is going to cease to exist. Now, I suspect it will take Jacob a couple of hours to find Baba Yaga and lure her into town. I suggest you all have something to eat and get some rest. This is probably going to be a long night."

After everyone had eaten what they could, Granny retired to her bedroom and Puck went to his. Uncle Jake went off in search of Baba Yaga, and Charming retreated into his mirror, leaving Mr. Canis and the girls alone.

The old man sat quietly, studying the girls. His face looked as if he were wrestling with a question. Sabrina knew what it would be and dreaded having to answer it. How do you tell someone he is going to be taken over by a monster and lose his soul?

"Can I do anything to stop it?" Mr. Canis asked finally, looking down at the sharp black talons on his hand.

"Yes!" Daphne said.

Sabrina, on the other hand, wasn't so sure. Canis had been creeping toward a complete metamorphosis since his fight with Rumpelstiltskin in the tunnels beneath the town several months ago. Nothing he had done since had slowed his change. Still, she knew it was best to keep her doubts to herself. "Our future selves believed we could change things, and we already have, a little."

"Do you know when it happens to me?" the old man asked.

The girls shook their heads. They should have asked when

they had the chance, but there were so many other questions that had gone unanswered too.

"Perhaps if I altered course I could stop it," Canis said. "That's what you're trying to do, correct?"

"We know we've changed a few things," Sabrina said. "Though we have no idea if it has made a difference in the future."

Canis got up from his chair. He repeated Granny Relda's advice about getting some rest and then slowly climbed the steps to his room.

"Are we going to lose him?" Daphne whispered.

"I don't know," Sabrina said.

After a few moments of silence, the girls went up to their room. Elvis padded along beside them and hopped up onto their bed.

"I guess we better get some rest," Daphne said, shutting off the light.

"I've got a bad feeling," Sabrina said.

"About tonight?"

"No, about the future, about this case. We still haven't found the missing items and it seems like things keep popping up to get in the way. What if we can't figure out who the thief is? What if we don't solve this mystery? What if there are things we can't change?"

The girls slipped their hands together and lay quietly. The darkness was like a heavy weight on their chests.

• • •

Sabrina awoke to an incredible shaking. Her head felt like it was going to bounce off her shoulders. The bed seemed to be moving around the room on its own. She looked over at her sister. Daphne had her eyes closed, concentrating hard. She also had the magic detector in her hand, and it was vibrating.

"Ugh, I think I'm going to be sick," Daphne said, squirming around the bed like someone had tossed a handful of worms down her pants.

"What's going on?" Sabrina asked, doing her best to keep the bed from careening into her father's desk.

"I feel like one of those time tears is about to open up again. Ohhh, my legs feel like pudding."

"Where is it going to happen? Can you tell?"

"There's going to be one in the river. It's going to be a big one too."

"Big enough for Wilhelm's ship?"

"Mucho big-o!"

The shimmering and shaking stopped, and Daphne shook her arms out as if they had fallen asleep. "We have to go now!"

Sabrina glanced over at the alarm clock on the night table by the bed.

"It's only ten o'clock. We can't go now. What about Uncle Jake? We don't know if he's found Baba Yaga yet!"

"This could be the only chance we get to send Wilhelm back," Daphne said as she put the magic detector into her pants pocket.

The girls leaped out of bed and raced into their grandmother's room. Granny Relda was still resting and they had to shake her from her nap.

"*Lieblings*, for heaven's sake!" Granny Relda cried as she sat up in bed.

"There's a time tear opening in the river soon. We need to go now."

"A time what?" the old woman said.

"A hole in time," Sabrina explained. "Just like the one Wilhelm came through to get here. We need to get him back on the boat so they can sail into it and get back to where they belong, but it has to happen soon."

"How do you know all this?"

"Granny, you keep secrets from us sometimes to protect us, right?" Daphne asked.

The old woman nodded.

"Well, this is our secret and you're just going to have to trust us, like we trust you."

Granny laughed. "But girls, you never trust me."

"Fine, then trust us like we're *supposed* to trust you," Sabrina said, pulling her grandmother out of bed and down the hallway. Meanwhile, Daphne pounded on Puck's door. The fairy joined them shortly, strapped with enough of his glop grenades to fight a war, and everyone rushed downstairs where Canis was sitting on the couch.

"We have to—" Granny started, but Mr. Canis held up his hand.

"I heard," he replied. "The car is already warmed up."

"What about Jacob?" Charming said as he poked his head out of his mirror.

"He's only been gone an hour and there's no way to reach him," Granny Relda said. "We're going to have to try something else."

Charming disappeared into his mirror and moments later returned, leading a brilliant white stallion out of the reflection. Even Canis, who was rarely surprised by anything, was stunned. Elvis looked up at the horse as if he were in the presence of royalty.

"I'll go for Jacob," the prince said as he led the horse outside. The rest of the group followed him. He mounted the creature and raced off into the night.

Daphne looked over at her grandmother with a smile. "Remember when you told me I couldn't have a pony because we didn't have enough room?"

Granny shook her head. "Not a chance."

Mr. Canis drove faster than he ever had. He whipped the old jalopy through the empty back roads, over the wooden bridges, and across the abandoned train tracks like he was an international race-car driver. Sabrina was happy he understood the urgency of their plan, but it was times like this she wished the car had more modern safety features. She tightened the ropes that the family had installed as makeshift seat belts around her waist. Even the usually fearless Puck put his on.

When they got to the town, Canis parked the car across from the police station and everyone got out.

"Puck, go ahead and take your position," Granny said.

Puck's wings spread out and flapped vigorously, lifting him into the air. "I'll wait for you at the dock," he said, and then zipped off toward the river.

Canis nodded. "What next?"

"Unfortunately, this plan of ours was somewhat dependent upon Jacob," Granny said. "We need to give Charming some time to find him and Baba Yaga."

"We can't wait another second," Daphne said as she pointed

to the sky. The stars seemed to have been devoured by a swirling black mass hovering high over the town. It was bigger and uglier than any Sabrina had seen before. "We've got to do this now, Granny."

"All right," their grandmother said. "I suppose we can sneak around the back and knock a hole in the wall. At least that much of the plan could still work."

"No, stop!" Mr. Canis said, sniffing the air. "There are men stationed on the top of the building and a large group of them at the back."

"How many do you think?" Granny said.

"I smell fifty of them, maybe more."

"They knew we were coming," Sabrina said, spotting one of the playing-card soldiers peering over the edge of the jailhouse roof. She also saw the deadly broadsword he held in his hands.

"I can take a few of them," Canis said. "But the three of you should wait here."

"Old friend, you'll never get past them all. This isn't going to work." The old woman sighed.

"Then what?"

"Then we go right through the front door," Sabrina said.

The family turned to her.

"Remember our escape training?" Sabrina said. "Puck knew

we would head for the woods so he didn't bother to guard the path. I bet you a million bucks Nottingham thinks the same way. He would never suspect us coming through the front door. I bet the inside isn't guarded at all!"

Her family and friends looked at her for a long time. Their faces were filled with doubt, but suddenly Mr. Canis started across the street. "Let's do it."

"What's the plan?" Granny asked as the rest of the family hurried to catch up to Canis.

"Mr. Canis can just run through and make us a path to the cell. We'll follow him."

"There's going to be a lot of dust, so stay close," the old man said, and then he bolted right through the front door. His face may have appeared old and frail, but he slammed through the offices like a powerful wrecking machine, plowing through walls, overturning desks, and making his own path to the jail cells at the back of the building. The women followed the best they could, dodging falling plaster and broken electrical lines. They held their faces under their shirts to filter out some of the debris. The blitz made a tremendous racket and would surely attract the attention of the guards outside, but Sabrina was right, Nottingham hadn't bothered to fortify the inside of the jail.

In no time, the group had reached the back of the building.

There they found Wilhelm locked inside a small cell. The poor man was terrified by what he had heard coming toward him. He leaped from his chair, lifted it, and waved it threateningly at the group.

"Zurück bleiben! Ich möchte Sie nicht verletzen!" Wilhelm shouted.

"What did he say?" Sabrina asked.

"He's frightened. He thinks we've come to hurt him," Granny explained, then turned to the man. "Wilhelm, it's us. We've come to rescue you."

"Rescue?" Wilhelm cried. He set his chair down on the ground and shook his jail cell bars as if to remind them of their next obstacle.

Canis reached for the bars. Using his incredible strength, he bent them apart, wrestling with them until there was an opening big enough for Wilhelm to step through.

Just then, Sabrina heard Nottingham's angry voice. "The prisoner is escaping, you fools!" he shouted. His furious bellowing was drowned out by the approaching feet of what sounded like four dozen guards.

"We've got to get out of here—now." Granny said.

Canis stepped to the back wall, pulled back his fist, and slammed it into the concrete. It crumbled, shaking the rafters. A

few cinder blocks completely collapsed, exposing the outside—and freedom—to the group. One more thump sent a spray of concrete and soot all over the room, but when the dust settled, there was a hole big enough for a seven-foot, three-hundred-pound man to step through.

"Everyone out!" Granny cried as she helped Sabrina and Daphne through the hole. Wilhelm and the old woman followed.

Before Mr. Canis could get through, Sabrina heard a sinister voice from inside the station.

"You do realize that breaking a prisoner out of jail is a big no-no," Nottingham said, and then she heard Mr. Canis roar in pain. The dust billowing out of the hole prevented her from seeing what was happening, but she knew he had been hurt badly. A moment later, Nottingham's ugly form stepped through the hole.

"I really should arrest you, Grimms, but I have a better way of solving our problem," he said as he reached for the crossbow strapped to his back. He loaded it with a steel arrow and leveled it at Wilhelm's chest. "One shot changes everything in this town, and though I know the throngs of people eager to see Wilhelm swing from the gallows will be disappointed, having their freedom will more than make up for missing the show."

And then he pulled the trigger.

10

t seemed to Sabrina that the arrow sailed across space in slow motion. She wondered what it would be like to suddenly not exist. Would they just blink into nothing, or would it feel like dying?

But the arrow never reached its target. Instead, there was a loud, quaking thump, which knocked everyone to the ground. As they scampered to their feet and realized Wilhelm was unharmed, they were confronted by the source of the thump. Baba Yaga had arrived in her horrifying house. The old crone was leaning out of her window with a glowing ball in her hand. It lit up like a firecracker and a blast of red energy hit Nottingham in the chest as he turned to face the witch.

"I want my wand!" she shouted.

The witch's magic tossed Nottingham several yards and

slammed him onto the ground. But a second later he still had the presence of mind to scamper behind a tree. "I don't know what you're talking about!"

The monstrous house raced toward him. One of its legs snatched the tree out of the ground, roots and all, leaving the sheriff vulnerable and panicked.

Wilhelm seemed quite disturbed by what he was seeing. He cried out something in German, but his message was clear. Sabrina's great-great-great-great-great-grandfather was completely freaked out.

"Baba Yaga's not going to be fooled for very long," Charming said as he rode up on his stallion.

Uncle Jake was right behind him, hovering on a flying carpet. "He's right. We should go."

Daphne nodded. "I agree. That storm is coming mucho fast-o."

"We can't leave! Mr. Canis is still in there," Sabrina said.

Just then the old man stepped through the hole. He held his hand to his left eye as blood seeped down his wrist.

"Old friend!" Granny gasped.

"It is nothing," the old man said, but his voice was pained.

Granny removed a handkerchief from her handbag and gave it to the old man. He held it to his wound and then ushered everyone around the building to the street. "We have to get to the boat."

The family raced the three blocks to the town marina. There they found Puck waiting impatiently.

"It's about time!" Puck said. "I'm dying of hunger."

"Is the boat ready?" the old woman asked.

"Naturally," Puck replied as he gestured to Wilhelm's tiny rowboat. Uncle Jake helped Granny Relda into it, then the girls, Wilhelm, and finally himself.

"You know what to do?" Uncle Jake asked the fairy boy.

"No sweat. This is going to be simple," Puck crowed as he shot into the sky. He had barely gotten aloft when he was nearly knocked out of the sky by a cannonball.

"They're shooting at us!" Daphne exclaimed.

Uncle Jake took the oars and rowed with all his might. They streaked across the river right toward the ship, while more cannon shots slammed into the water around them.

"They must think we're coming to attack," Granny said.

Wilhelm leaped from his seat and waved at the boat. His excitement nearly capsized them, and Sabrina had to brace herself to keep from falling in the river. His wild gestures made her nervous. It seemed like he was just making them an easier target.

There were two more shots, but then the explosions stopped

altogether, giving them smooth sailing to the side of the ship. Uncle Jake and Wilhelm helped Granny aboard and then the girls scampered up on their own power.

Once aboard, Sabrina was stunned by the people who surrounded her. Nearly everyone she had ever met from the town was there: Briar Rose; Mr. Seven and the rest of the seven dwarfs; Ms. White; Beauty and her husband, the Beast; and even some old enemies like Jack the Giant Killer and Rumpelstiltskin. She stepped in front of her family and clenched her fists, prepared to fight their way off the ship, but then it dawned on her that no one knew who they were.

Wilhelm said something in German that seemed to calm the nerves of the passengers.

"What did he say?" Sabrina asked.

"He said that he is OK, but there has been an odd turn of events," Granny explained. Then she turned to the rest of the crowd. "I know many of you are confused. You set sail for America expecting to find a relatively unsettled plot of land. Well, you found America. You just didn't show up at the right time."

"What are you talking about, old woman?" Beast growled. "And who are you?"

"My name is Relda Grimm, and the town you see before you is Ferryport Landing. It's your home, or at least it will be. You've slipped through a tear in time. You're more than two hundred years in the future."

Several people cried out in shock while others rushed to the sides of the ship to gawk out at the little town.

"Wilhelm was taken against his will, but we have returned him," Granny continued.

"Did you say your name is Grimm?" Snow White asked as she stepped from the crowd. She was as beautiful as ever.

"Yes," Granny replied. "This is my son, Jacob, and my grand-daughters, Sabrina and Daphne."

The Everafters on the boat roared with approval. "Our savior's family lives on!" a woman said from the back of the crowd. Sabrina peered back and was stunned to find it was the Queen of Hearts cheering for her.

"Times sure have changed," she grumbled.

"Are we friends?" Ms. White asked the family.

Granny smiled. "You're one of our best friends, Snow. I wish that I could explain more, but there is no time. We have to get you back where you belong."

Suddenly, Daphne began to vibrate again. "That will be any minute now," the little girl said.

"We need to get off this boat unless we want to join them in the past," Sabrina added.

"Now!" Puck said, as he buzzed the boat. "Do I do it now?"

"Just a moment, Puck," Granny said, then turned back to the passengers. "It was a pleasure to meet you all, but we really must go."

Uncle Jacob took Briar Rose by the hand. "I'll see you in two hundred years."

The beautiful princess looked confused, but gave him one of her goofy smiles.

Uncle Jake led Granny back to the side of the ship and did his best to help her down. It wasn't as easy as climbing aboard.

"Let my friends help you," Cinderella said. She took three small brown mice from her pocket and set them on the ground. Sabrina watched as they morphed into full-grown men, and once the change was complete she immediately recognized them. They were Malcolm, Alexander, and Bradford—the men who worked on her radio show. They helped the family off the ship and down into the rowboat.

"Now?" Puck said impatiently.

"Now!" Uncle Jake cried once they were safely rowing back toward the shore.

Sabrina watched as Puck pulled the pins on his glop grenades and launched them onto the deck of the ship. They exploded, but not in a wave of disgusting filth like usual. These grenades were filled with a soft pink dust that covered the passengers. Sabrina recognized it as Forgetful Dust, and though she knew it was necessary to wipe the memories of everyone on the *New Beginning* so that history couldn't be altered, she still regretted the opportunity they were giving up. They had a chance to change some of the things that made life in Ferryport Landing so hard. Maybe they could have stopped the uprising that led to the barrier's construction. Maybe they could have changed the hatred so many of the Everafters felt for the Grimms. The possibilities were endless. She watched as the passengers stood on the sides of the boat, glassy eyed. The Beast and his wife, the Frog Prince, Little Bo Peep, Morgan le Fay, Cinderella and her mice assistants looked back at them, and then the ship was gone, swirling into the nothingness of the storm that hovered above. But in its wake Sabrina finally understood who had stolen the magical items.

"I just solved the case!" she shouted, leaping up from her seat. She was so excited she fell overboard into the cold water. Uncle Jake snatched her by the sleeve and pulled her back into the boat.

"Sabrina! Are you OK?"

"I've solved the mystery!" she said as she wiped water out of her eyes. "I know who stole the magic items. It was Cinderella!"

"I don't believe it!" Daphne gasped.

"She came to her house with her husband, Tom. She must have brought her mice friends, and they snuck into the witches' bags," Sabrina said in a rush. "That's how they got into everyone's homes. They went as mice and turned into men to steal the objects. You saw them on the boat. They can shape-shift!"

"That explains the locker at Frau Pfefferkuchenhaus's office," Daphne added. "She must have stuck her bag inside and trapped one of them in there. He turned into a man and was able to kick the door open from the inside."

"But why? Why would Dr. Cindy need to steal this stuff?" Uncle Jake asked as he rowed the little boat to shore. "You heard her husband. The radio show is going national. They're going to be rich. They don't need to steal anything."

"I say we ask Dr. Cindy ourselves!" Granny Relda said as they reached the dock. Mr. Canis was there, waiting to help everyone back onto shore. His handkerchief was stained through with blood from his eye injury.

"Baba Yaga has nearly demolished the police station," Mr. Canis informed them. "It won't be long before she moves on to her next target."

"Not to worry, old friend," Granny said as Uncle Jake helped her out of the boat. "I think we know who has her wand."

The family rushed down the street to the radio station. On top of the building was a huge metal tower with a red light, and above that, there was another of the frightening time storms. They pushed through the doors of WFPR and headed for the stairs, where a sign read STUDIO—3RD FLOOR. But before they reached the first step, they were stopped in their tracks by a huge security guard.

"Can I help you?" he said, though his tone sounded not at all helpful.

"We need to talk to Dr. Cindy," Granny Relda explained.

"Well, she's on the air right now, so I suggest you give her a call."

"You don't understand," Sabrina said. "She's doing something very dangerous!"

"Like listening to callers whine about their miserable lives?" the security guard said sarcastically. He reached down and turned a knob on a radio. Dr. Cindy was indeed on the air, trying to help a woman understand that she would never find happiness in food.

"Now, like I said, she's busy," the security guard said roughly. He opened the door and ushered everyone back outside.

"Something's going on up there," Daphne said. "I can feel it." The magic detector was nearly bouncing out of her hand.

"Maybe Mr. Canis could eat the guard," Puck said.

Canis shrugged as if that wasn't such a bad idea.

"I don't think we need to eat anyone," Sabrina said, turning to Puck and studying the arsenal of glop grenades he had strapped to his chest. "Got any of those with real glop in them?"

Puck smiled.

Uncle Jake propped the door open just a crack. Puck pulled the pin on a grenade and Sabrina tossed it inside. A second later there was a loud splat and the security guard came running outside, covered in a funky-smelling goo.

"I'm going to be sick," he cried, rolling around on the ground. With the guard incapacitated, the family rushed back inside the station and hurried up the steps.

Moments later, they stormed through a door with a sign above it that flashed ON AIR. Dr. Cindy was sitting at a desk with a big microphone hanging from the ceiling above her. She was wearing a pair of headphones and sipping on coffee while she talked to her caller. She looked up in shock when the group barged in, then leaned in to her mike. "Folks, I think we need to break for a commercial. We'll be right back with more of *The Dr. Cindy Show* in just a moment."

The On Air light went dim and Dr. Cindy took off her headphones. "What's going on? I'm doing a show."

"We know what you've been up to," Sabrina said, unconvinced by the woman's dumbfounded expression. "We know all about it."

"I have no idea what you're talking about," Cindy said.

"The magic items!" Daphne said. "Merlin's Wand, the Wonder Clock, the water from the Fountain of Youth. We know you stole them."

"Stole them? I've never stolen anything in my life," Cindy exclaimed. "Relda, I don't know what's going on, but this is incredibly rude, letting your grandchildren come in here and accuse me of being a criminal."

"Cindy, I would agree if we didn't have proof. We know you sent your assistants to break into people's homes. They snuck in as mice and then transformed back into men once they found what they were looking for."

"But you don't know what you're doing," Uncle Jake added. "We know you're trying to combine the items to make some new kind of magic, but it's not working, and you're causing chaos all over town. You have to stop before, well, I don't know before what, but it could be really bad."

Cindy was horrified. "I never sent my assistants anywhere to do any such thing."

"Then let's ask them ourselves. Where are they?" Mr. Canis said. "I know ways of making them admit their guilt."

"They're on the roof," Dr. Cindy said. "During the broadcast, something went wrong with the transmitter and they're trying to fix it. My husband, Tom, is up there supervising the repairs."

"Let's go have a conversation with them, then," Granny said.

Cindy stormed past the group in a huff. She led them up a flight of steps and onto the roof. As she threw open the door the group was blinded by a penetrating blue light.

Sabrina had to shield her eyes just to see two feet in front of her, but soon her sight adjusted and what she saw was shocking. Cindy's husband, Tom Baxter, was standing at the base of the radio tower. He was holding an ornate wooden clock in his hands. Malcolm, the producer, stood nearby with what appeared to be a tiny vial of water. Alexander was blasting the vial with a magic wand, causing the rays of energy from the wand to pass through the fluid and onto Tom. Bradford monitored the storm above, shouting information to the others about its size and shape. From the looks of the power coming out of the wand, the energy should have obliterated Tom Baxter, but the magic bounced off the magnificent clock, circling Tom in snakelike blue lights. Behind him was an even more shocking sight. There was an open black hole like the ones Sabrina had seen in the skies during the other storms. She knew it was a tear in the fabric of time itself.

"Tom!" Cindy shouted. "What is going on here?"

Tom's face changed from happiness to concern. "Go back downstairs, Cindy. This is very dangerous. It's not safe for you to be up here."

"What are you doing, Tom?" the radio host cried.

Tom smiled. His yellow eyes lit up when he looked at his young wife. "I'm giving us a future," he said.

"It's happening," Malcolm shouted.

Suddenly, there was an immense blast from the wand and Tom's body was pushed back to the surface of the black hole. He hovered there as the powerful vacuum behind him began to pull things in. At first it was just a few stray leaves, but Sabrina could feel the energy building. She studied Tom closely, wondering why he wasn't afraid, and then she began to see subtle changes in his appearance. His gray head started to sprout new, brown hair.

"You have to stop this," Granny yelled.

"Don't worry, we've got this under control," Bradford replied. "It'll all be over soon."

Sabrina glanced at the storm swirling above. "Mr. Baxter, whatever you're doing has some nasty side-effects. It's causing tears in time!" she shouted over the noise.

"Yes, I know," Tom yelled, as the pronounced stoop in his posture corrected itself. "I hope they weren't too much of an inconvenience.

It took us a while to get the proper devices to build my machine."

"What is this?" Cindy asked.

"It's a time machine, and it's too dangerous," Granny said.

Tom smiled. "Relda, I didn't build a time machine. I built a clock. A clock that allows me to roll back the years on myself."

"Uh-oh," Daphne said as the magic detector started to shake violently. She pointed to the black hole as it grew nearly ten times in size. Worse, Sabrina saw something begin to descend from it. Slipping through the surface was a dragon. It huffed and then darted clear out of the blackness, flying into the air with a head-splitting roar.

"That was the coolest thing I've ever seen," Puck said as he pulled his little wooden sword from his waist and released his wings. "I'm going to kill it."

"You're going to get plenty of practice when you get older," Sabrina said as she pulled on his sleeve.

Puck frowned at her. "What do you mean by that? I'm an Everafter. I don't get older!" he said, though his voice cracked on several of the words. He held his throat in shock.

The dragon buzzed the building, leaving a trail of sulfurous fumes in its wake. Sabrina had to dive to get out of the way of its sharp claws and long tail.

"Mr. Baxter, you have to stop this. You've already let something out that could kill us all," Uncle Jake shouted. "What's next?"

Tom shook his head. "It won't be long now," he said as his yellow eyes grew bright and clear. The dark spots on his skin faded and his stringy arms and legs grew lean and muscular.

Cindy rushed to him and stood as close as the energy swirling around him would allow. "Why are you doing this?"

"Because I love you, Doc. I have always loved you, and I always will, but I am only a man and you are an Everafter. My body is withering away. I've grown too feeble to even take you on a picnic or dance to our wedding song. In no time at all I would have been gone. You will never die, Cindy. Now, neither will I."

Cindy cried out to him to stop, but her eyes were filled with wonder and possibility. "I love you."

"You better, Cinderella, 'cause now you're stuck with me forever," Tom said as he stepped down from the black portal. The blue energy that had once enveloped him was gone, as were his wrinkles. He was no longer old. Now he was young, strong, and handsome. He didn't look a day over twenty-five. He took Cindy in his arms and kissed her. "It's over, darling."

But Tom Baxter was wrong. The dragon flying overhead let out an angry roar and a series of flaming assaults. The first one hit the transmitting tower, and it fell over like a child's toy. Its steel girders melted into liquid and poured all over the roof. Everyone scrambled to get out of the way. The next blast from the dragon missed them and hit a parked car on the street below.

"Uh-oh," Daphne said as the magic detector began to shimmer again.

"What?" Sabrina asked. "Is something else coming through the hole?"

Before Daphne could answer, Tom was violently yanked backward to the edge of the black tear. He squirmed to break free but couldn't. Worse still, the hole began to grow at an alarming rate, along with its gravitational pull. The black tear was no longer satisfied with leaves or loose paper; it was pulling at everything.

"Boys, what's going on?" Tom called to his assistants.

Malcolm, Alexander, and Bradford stumbled back in fear. "We didn't do this!" Alexander shouted.

"Can you pull yourself free?" Cindy said as she rushed to her husband. He shook his head. She reached up and took his hand, desperately trying to pull him off the hole's edge, but she wasn't strong enough. She even lost a little gold bracelet as it sailed off her wrist and disappeared into the void.

"I guess it's not going to let me go," Tom said, forcing a little laugh. "Honey, you might be married to a teenager pretty soon."

Cindy turned to the family. "Do something!" she begged.

Uncle Jake was already fumbling through his pockets. He pulled out one trinket after another, examined them, and shoved them back into his jacket. "I don't think I've got anything that can stop this."

"Any suggestions?" Sabrina asked her grandmother. Granny's handbag was already swinging toward the hole.

"Perhaps the three of you should go down to the street where it is safe."

"Aww, I want to see what happens," Puck complained.

The fallen tower began to roll toward the time hole. Canis grabbed Granny and the girls and leaped over it as it rushed toward them like a stampeding rhino. Luckily, Uncle Jake was not in its path and Puck simply rose into the air to avoid it. A second later the entire transmitter was sucked into the tear.

Unfortunately, as Puck rose off the ground he found himself trapped in the black hole's gravitational pull. He flapped his wings hard in an effort to escape, but there was nothing for him to grab onto. He drifted closer and closer to the emptiness with nothing to stop him. "Uh, we've got a problem," he said.

Sabrina grabbed his foot as he passed, but she too was pulled up. "Help!" she yelled. Daphne latched on to her as well and soon the three of them were right below the massive hole in time.

"Children!" Granny cried as she held on for dear life to the side of the building.

But she was too far away to be of any help, as were Mr. Canis and Uncle Jake, and slowly Puck began to drift into the blackness. His face and upper torso were soon gone, then his waist and finally his knees. All that was left in this world of the boy fairy was his sneakers, which Sabrina clung to with all her strength.

"I'm losing him!" she cried in desperation. "Puck, you have to fight it!"

Without warning, the hole quadrupled in size, threatening to swallow the entire building. From inside it something unexpected appeared—an enormous house sitting on top of two grotesque chicken legs. The house pushed the children back through the hole and blocked most of the suction pulling everything toward the time tear. But it wasn't Baba Yaga inside. Sabrina could see her older self hovering in the window. When the house cleared the horizon of the hole, it planted itself on top of the radio station's roof. The door flew open and the older Sabrina, Daphne, and Puck ran out. The older Granny Relda wheeled herself out behind them.

"Dear me," Granny said as she studied the strange visitors.

"You've got to close this hole!" the older Daphne shouted as she raced to her younger self. Sabrina studied her; there was something different. She still wore Uncle Jake's coat, but the scar that had once marred her beautiful face was gone.

"How?" Daphne asked.

"Destroy the machine!" the older Granny Relda shouted over the raging storm.

Sabrina raced over to Malcolm, Alexander, and Bradford. They had lost control of the wand, which was floating on its own and still showering the vial of water and the clock with its power. Sabrina tried to grab it, but there was a shock and her hand felt like it was on fire.

"Don't touch it, child!" Tom shouted. "If you destroy it, you'll reverse the process."

Daphne reached for the vial of water with similar results. She cried out, which caused Cindy to look back at the girls. When she saw the pain in Daphne's face, it seemed to open her eyes to the rest of the chaos. Without a word, she picked up the Wonder Clock, lifted it over her head, and brought it down hard on the ground. It splintered into thousands of pieces. The wand suddenly stopped firing and the wind disappeared. Tom fell from the surface of the hole as it began to shrink.

"Cindy! Why? " he cried, though his voice sounded weak and tired.

"I don't need you to be young," she said as she stepped over to him and caressed his face. Sabrina could see he was returning to his normal age. His strong arms and legs had returned to feebleness and his back stooped.

"I did this so we could be together."

Cinderella looked into his eyes. "Then so be it," she whispered, and her body began to age as well. Her long blond hair turned white, wrinkles weaved across her perfect face, and her delicate hands became gnarled.

"Cindy, no!" Tom cried. "You can't go back. If you age you won't ever be young again."

"What would life be without you, my prince?" Cindy said, her voice rough and crackling. "When we say our good-byes I want to be by your side."

Sabrina's attention turned to the future Puck, who stepped up to the younger one. "Hello, Trickster King," he said.

Puck gaped at his older self.

"Try to be nicer to Sabrina," the grown-up Puck said with a chuckle. "She's going to be important to you in the future, and trust me, she'll never forgive you for gluing her head to that basketball."

Puck grinned. "I never glued her head to a basketball."

"You're giving him ideas!" the older Sabrina said reproachfully.

Mr. Canis and Granny Relda stepped forward. Granny seemed

stunned by her older self, but Canis walked up to her and took her hand.

"It's good to see you, old friend," the older Granny said.

"I know what happens, I just don't know when," he said.

"You don't have a lot of time left," the old woman said before breaking into a coughing fit.

"How do I stop it?"

"You can't," the future Granny Relda said. "I'm sorry."

"All right, folks, the hole is getting pretty small," the older Puck said. "If we are going home, we better get going."

"Those with me, get back in the house," the future Daphne said. "The rest, get down." Everyone did as they were told. Then the older Daphne fired a wand into the air. It got the attention of the dragon, who made a beeline for the house. The older Daphne turned to little Daphne and smiled.

"There's big things ahead, girl. You're going to have to grow up a little," she said.

"I'll try!" Daphne called back.

Her future self darted into the house with her companions, and the house lumbered back into the black hole. The dragon roared, launched another ball of fire at it, and then disappeared into the abyss as well. A second later, the storm was gone and the hole in time closed in on itself.

• • •

Sabrina's twelfth birthday was embarrassing. Granny Relda made a big deal out of it, forcing her to wear a funny hat that read BIRTHDAY GIRL!

Daphne gave Sabrina her princess tiara. Uncle Jake gave her a new pair of sneakers. Mr. Canis, who was now wearing a bandage on his wounded eye, bought her a little portable radio for her room, and Granny showered her with clothes and a new bicycle. Puck left a box on the kitchen table with her name on it. Inside, she found a basketball and a tube of industrial-strength glue with a note that read IT'S COMING WHEN YOU LEAST EXPECT IT.

"Where is the freak baby, anyway?" Sabrina asked.

"In his room pouting," Granny Relda said. "He's not at all happy about his current growth spurt."

"Is he sick?" Daphne asked.

"No, he's growing up," Granny said.

"And if you think he's a pain now, wait until he starts getting pimples," Uncle Jake said.

Prince Charming also attended the party, indulging in Granny's German Chocolate Cake. There was music, laughter, and happiness, which had been in short supply as of late. It seemed as if their recent troubles with taxes, Mayor Heart, and

Nottingham would soon be distant memories.

There was a knock at the door. "Who can that be?" Granny said.

"That's Sabrina's birthday present," Charming said.

Sabrina was surprised. "You got me a birthday present?"

"Go answer the door," he said.

A million ideas raced through her mind. What could the prince have gotten her? She threw open the door and was a little startled to find a strange woman standing on the porch. She was thin with brown hair and a pale complexion. Her lips were full and her eyes green. She wore a little black dress, pearls, and high-heeled shoes, and she oozed sophistication. Sabrina knew only one person that was more beautiful than this woman and that was Snow White.

"Are you Sabrina Grimm?" she asked.

Sabrina nodded.

"My name is Bunny Lancaster," she said. "William sent me."

"OK," Sabrina said, a little dopey. "Are you my present?"

The woman cocked an eyebrow. "I'm not sure what you mean, dear."

Charming appeared at the door. "Bunny, thank you for coming. Please come in."

The woman entered and the family gathered around her.

"Mrs. Grimm, this is Bunny Lancaster," Charming said.

"I know who she is," the old woman said coolly. Sabrina had never seen her grandmother react that way to anyone. Where was the smile? Where was the sweet hello?

"Are you an Everafter?" Daphne asked, rushing to shake the woman's hand. She had her own palm prepped and ready to bite.

Bunny nodded.

"Which one?" Daphne asked, barely able to contain her excitement.

Bunny shifted uncomfortably. "In some circles I have the rather unfortunate title of the Wicked Queen."

Daphne went for the bite but then stopped. "You mean the one that tried to kill Snow White?"

"I didn't try to kill her," Bunny said softly.

"Well, Mr. Charming. Thank you for the birthday present, but you shouldn't have. Really, you shouldn't have," Sabrina said.

"I know this is uncomfortable, but Bunny is here to help you," Charming said.

"Help me?"

"Take me to your mirror," the Wicked Queen replied.

"Uh, I'm not sure what you mean," Granny stammered.

"Mrs. Grimm, I am fully aware that you possess a magic mirror," the woman said impatiently. "I also know that Snow voluntarily gave it to your family nearly a hundred years ago. I would like to see it."

Granny glanced at Charming, who nodded as if to say Bunny could be trusted. Then she took out the set of keys from her handbag and led the group upstairs. She unlocked the door to the mirror's room, and everyone stepped inside. When the door closed, the roaring began.

"WHO DARES INVADE MY SANCTUARY!" Mirror's violent face filled the reflection.

"Control yourself," the Wicked Queen said.

"Bunny? Is that you?" Mirror asked.

There was a raw silence between the two. They shared an angry and uncomfortable look.

"What a pleasant surprise," Mirror said, forcing a smile to his face.

The Wicked Queen stepped forward. "Mirror, Mirror can you tell, how to break the sleeping spell?"

"Right down to business, Bunny? Very well, a kiss is all it takes," Mirror said.

"That's not what I asked, servant," the woman said sternly. Sabrina bristled at the way the woman was talking to her friend. Mirror shifted, obviously taken aback by the queen's rude tone.

"Bunny, I—"

"Mirror, are you arguing with me?"

"No, I'm—"

"I asked you a question."

"And I answered it," Mirror said.

"No, you did not! Any fool knows a romantic kiss will break a sleeping spell. Do you think I don't know it? I invented this spell. I also know that there is always a back door. What is the back door?"

"I'm not sure what you mean?"

The Wicked Queen's right hand began to glow red. Its intensity was blinding and heat came off it like the fireballs the dragon had shot at them the night before. "Mrs. Grimm, your mirror is defective. Allow me to fix it for you."

"Wait, what are you planning on doing?" Sabrina shouted.

"The repairs will not harm the contents, but this sorry excuse for a guardian is damaged. I take great pride in my work, and I should have fixed it a long time ago."

"Bunny, don't do anything you'll regret!" Mirror said.

"You pompous, ridiculous little joke," the Wicked Queen said as she placed her red hand on the surface of the mirror. "It's not like I'm going to kill you. You don't exist. You are a creation, a puppet, a shadow of a person. Your job is to serve your master, and you are failing. When a question is asked you are to answer it clearly and thoroughly. You need to be repaired."

Mirror cried out in pain.

"Leave him alone!" Daphne shouted.

Angry clouds began to gather around Mirror's head. "You are not my master."

"Every walking and talking person in the world is your master," Bunny said quietly. "I created you. I know what the rules are. Now, I'm going to ask you again and this time I want you to give me a thorough answer. Mirror, Mirror, can you tell, how to break the sleeping spell?"

Mirror curled his lip and looked embarrassed. Sabrina wasn't happy either. Mirror was her friend and she didn't like strangers being mean to her friends. She was fully prepared to step between the two of them when the Wicked Queen took her hand off the mirror's reflection, leaving a bright red handprint that quickly faded away. As it disappeared, so did Mirror's face, and another image replaced it. Sitting in a café on a cobblestone street was a blond woman with short, curly hair. She was sipping coffee and writing in a journal as a waiter in black pants and a white apron tried to get her attention. He smiled at her and said something funny, but she seemed to be in her own little world.

"There's your answer," the Wicked Queen said.

"Who's that?" Daphne asked.

"Goldilocks," Uncle Jake whispered.

"Goldilocks," Granny repeated.

"Goldilocks indeed," Bunny said, eyeing each member of the Grimm family suspiciously. "It seems as if she has found a way out of our happy little town. Lucky, lucky girl."

"Bunny, I appreciate the help," Charming said as he escorted her out of the room.

"Is she the one Dad was in love with before he met Mom?" Sabrina asked.

Granny shuffled her feet.

"Tell her, Mom," Uncle Jake said. "It's her birthday."

"Well, is she the one?"

Granny nodded. "Yes. Now, let's say good-bye to our guest."

Everyone piled out of the room except Sabrina. Mirror's face appeared in the reflection. He looked as if he had just been in a prizefight. "Starfish—"

"Have you known all along?" Sabrina said, her voice trembling with anger and hurt.

Mirror shook his head. "No. That's not how it works. I don't *know* anything."

"Were you keeping it from us?" She felt like a volcano bubbling over with emotion.

"It's hard to explain, Sabrina. If the question isn't specific, the answers don't come to me. I'm not omnipotent. I'm just a magic mirror, and I do what I was made to do. Ask a question. Get an answer. If I had known there were more answers, I would have told you. Bunny forgets that I wasn't one of the deluxe mirrors. I was the first, the test product. She forgets she didn't give me all the bells and whistles she gave the others."

Through her anger, Sabrina could hear the pain in Mirror's voice. It made her feel sorry for him, and her rage faded away. "It's OK," she said. "There is nothing wrong with you. Don't let her get to you."

Mirror looked as if he might cry. His face faded from the reflection.

Sabrina looked down at her mother and father, still slumbering soundly in the queen-size bed in the center of the room. "Now all we have to do is find Goldilocks," she said.

She joined everyone at the bottom of the stairs. Bunny was saying her farewells, though Granny and Mr. Canis were keeping their distance. She turned and opened the door. Standing on the porch was Snow White. The teacher was so stunned, she dropped a glass carousel she was carrying, cracking it into several pieces.

"Snow," Bunny said.

"Mother," Snow replied as if in shock.

"Mother!" the girls shouted in unison.

"Billy?" Ms. White cried when she noticed Prince Charming through the doorway. She looked back and forth at all of them, confused. "Where have you been?"

"I've been busy," Charming said coolly. Sabrina was shocked at his attitude, but she knew the prince didn't want to see Ms. White. He said he was hiding from her to protect her. Being aloof must be part of the plan.

"I've been worried," Ms. White stammered. "I left messages. I've searched for you."

"Then you're a fool," Charming said. "You think I would want you? You left me at the altar. You humiliated me in front of my family and friends."

"Billy!"

"Go home, Snow. You're embarrassing yourself."

Sabrina expected the teacher to turn and run off in tears, but instead she reached back and socked Charming in the jaw. He stood his ground, but it was obvious he was in pain.

"You sorry excuse for a man!" Ms. White said. "How could I have been so blind?" Then she turned on Granny Relda. "And you! Now you're befriending my mother? I thought we were better friends than that. You of all people know what she has done."

"Snow, I didn't—"

"And you've been hiding Billy here all along while I suffered?"

Granny never got a chance to explain. The lovely woman stormed down the porch steps and raced off in her car before anyone could stop her.

"Well, that's another party I've ruined," Bunny muttered. She waved her hand over the broken carousel and it instantly reassembled, looking brand-new. She handed it to Sabrina. "Happy birthday, kid."

Moments later she got into a beautiful black sports car and sped away.

Charming walked across the room, picked up his huge full-length magic mirror, and carried it outside.

"Where are you going?" Granny Relda said. "You don't have to leave."

"I have things to do, Mrs. Grimm," he said. "And so does your family. You need to make sure Baba Yaga restores her guardians. You must make her understand that she is vulnerable."

"That's not going to be so easy," Uncle Jake said. "When I gave her back the wand she claimed that my family was now her mortal enemy for lying to her."

"She's moody," Charming said. "Find a way." Then he turned to the girls. "I have one more present for you, Sabrina, one to share with your sister. It's advice. No matter what the cost, save the ones you love. When you look back on me, remember these words. Remember why I did what I had to do."

He looked over to Mr. Canis and then back at the girls. "And get that weapon as soon as you can."

Sabrina was confused. She wanted to ask him what he meant, but he walked down to the street carrying his mirror and moments later he was gone.

• • •

That night, Sabrina was once again roused from sleep by incessant knocking on the front door. Later she would wonder why she had answered the door at all. It seemed as if every time she opened it, she got a nasty surprise. But it was late, and no one else in her family seemed to have heard the visitor. How could she have known that Nottingham and Mayor Heart would be on the other side? How could she have known that both of them would have bloodred handprints painted on their chests—the mark of the Scarlet Hand?

"So, you're with them," Sabrina said.

Mayor Heart looked down at the mark. "It is quite an honor to be able to follow the Master. He has great plans for this world."

Granny and Uncle Jake joined her at the door.

"I've got good news for you, Relda," Heart continued. "We've decided to let you keep your house—for now. I have a feeling we could have raised the tax to a billion dollars and you would still have found a way to pay it. So, congratulations, you are now the last human family in Ferryport Landing. Unfortunately, I have some bad news as well. You see, I tried to be nice and let you leave on your own. But you refused, so now I have to get mean. Nottingham, arrest Canis!"

Nottingham took a pair of handcuffs from his pants pocket. "Absolutely!"

"Your family has hidden behind Canis for decades. He's been the only thing between you and an angry mob on more than one occasion. I suspect that things will get very unpleasant for you if he isn't around."

"It was my idea to break into the jail and free Wilhelm," Granny said. "Arrest me instead."

"Oh, you think we're arresting him for a reason. How funny," Nottingham said with a laugh.

"You can't arrest an innocent person," Sabrina said.

"Fine!" Nottingham said. "I'm arresting him for murder."

"Murder?" Sabrina cried.

"The Big Bad Wolf murdered a little girl's grandmother," Nottingham said. "Perhaps you've heard this story?"

"Red Riding Hood," Uncle Jake said.

"Now, where is the old fleabag? If you're hiding him, I'll take you all in."

Mr. Canis appeared at the doorway. "I'll go with you, Nottingham," he said calmly and stepped out of the house. He had no fear or anger in his face. In fact, he seemed at peace.

The sheriff slapped his handcuffs on Canis's huge hands. "You've got the right to remain silent—" he started.

"You're just giving up?" Sabrina said to Canis. "You could run off. They'd never catch you."

"We all have our destinies, little one," Canis said. "Perhaps I can save everyone from mine."

"Whatzgoinon?" Daphne said as she came down the stairs. She was still rubbing the sleep from her eyes.

Sabrina stepped forward. "You won't get away with this. We'll stop you just like we've stopped all of the Scarlet Hand. We've got a whole family. There are only two of you."

"I'm afraid I disagree, child," a voice said from behind the mayor and Nottingham. Sabrina peered into the dark and saw a mob of Everafters stepping onto their lawn. At their forefront was the Beast, followed by the Frog Prince and his wife. Miss Muffet was one of them, as was her husband, the spider. Tweedledee and Tweedledum were there, accompanied by the Cheshire Cat. There was a sea of ogres, witches, trolls, cyclops, tree gnomes, leprechauns, and dozens of talking animals. There were Everafters Sabrina had seen all over town. Some she had spoken to, others had waited on her at local stores. Glinda the Good Witch stood with them. All had the same red handprint on their chests.

"You look surprised, Grimms. I was hoping you would be," Mayor Heart replied.

"Not surprised," Sabrina said. "Relieved, now I know which of you are the scum and which aren't."

"Oh, but you haven't met our latest recruit. Allow me to introduce the newest foot solider in the Scarlet Hand." The Grimms turned to look.

"I'm sure you'll agree he's just a prince of a guy," Nottingham added, and the crowd erupted into laughter.

And then Prince William Charming stepped to the front of the crowd and stood between Mayor Heart and Nottingham. His shirt was marked with a bloodred handprint.

To be continued in

THE SISTERS GRIMM

BOOK SIX: TALES FROM THE HOOD

ABOUT THE AUTHOR

Michael Buckley is the *New York Times* bestselling author of the *Sisters Grimm* and *NERDS* series. He has also written and developed television shows for many networks. Michael lives in Brooklyn, New York, with his wife, Alison, and his son, Finn.

This book was designed by Jay Colvin and Vivian Cheng, and art directed by Chad W. Beckerman. It is set in Adobe Garamond, a typeface that is based on those created in the sixteenth century by Claude Garamond. Garamond modeled his typefaces on those created by Venetian printers at the end of the fifteenth century. The modern version used in this book was designed by Robert Slimbach, who studied Garamond's historic typefaces at the Plantin-Moretus Museum in Antwerp, Belgium.

The capital letters at the beginning of each chapter are set in Daylilies, designed by Judith Sutcliffe. She created the typeface by decorating Goudy Old Style capitals with lilies.

Enjoy this sneak peek at

TALES FROM THE HOOD

BOOK SIX IN THE *SISTERS GRIMM* SERIES

Sabrina washed her face and was about to shut off the light and go back to bed when she heard something bubbling in the toilet. The lid was down and she couldn't see what was causing the noise, but she had her suspicions. Before Puck moved in with the family, he had lived in the woods for a decade. So modern conveniences mesmerized him—none more so than the toilet. He loved to flush it over and over and watch the water swirl down the hole and disappear. For months he was convinced that toilets were some kind of magic, until Uncle Jake explained how indoor plumbing worked. Unfortunately, this knowledge only increased Puck's interest, and it wasn't long before he was conducting what he called "scientific research" to discover what could be flushed down the tubes. It started out with a little loose change, but the items quickly grew in size: marbles, wristwatches, doorknobs, balls of yarn, even scoops of butter pecan ice cream swirled and disappeared. Granny finally put an end to it all when she caught Puck trying to flush a beaver he had trapped by the river. Ever since, the toilet had been coughing up Puck's "experiments." Last week Sabrina found one of her mittens inside. Now, apparently, something else was making its way to the surface. She bent down and lifted the lid, hoping it was the missing television remote control, which had vanished months ago.

But it wasn't the remote control. Instead it was something so shocking she would have nightmares about it the rest of her life and an unnatural fear of toilets in general. Who would expect to lift the toilet lid and find a little man sitting inside?

"Who goes there?" he said in a squeaky voice. He was no more than a foot tall and wore a tiny green suit, a green bowler hat, and shiny black shoes with bright brass buckles. His long red beard dipped into the toilet water.

Sabrina shrieked and slammed the toilet lid down on the creature's head. The little man groaned and shouted a few angry curses, but Sabrina didn't stick around to hear them. She was already running down the hallway, screaming for her grandmother.

Granny Relda stumbled out of her room. She was wearing an ankle-length nightgown and a sleeping cap that hid her gray hair. She looked the picture of the perfect grandmother, except, of course, for the sharpened battle-ax she held in her hand.

"*Liebling*!" her grandmother cried in a light German accent. *Liebling* was the German word for *sweetheart*. "What is going on?"

"There's a person in the toilet!" Sabrina said.

"A what?"

Before she could answer, Uncle Jake came out of a room at the end of the hall. He was fully dressed in jeans, leather boots, and a long overcoat with hundreds of little pockets sewn into it. He looked exhausted and in dire need of a shave. "What's all the hubbub about?"

"Sabrina says she saw something in the toilet," Granny Relda explained.

"I swear I flushed," Uncle Jake said as he threw up his hands.

"Not that! A person!" Sabrina shouted. "He spoke to me."

"Mom, you've really got to cut back on all the spicy food you've been feeding the girls," Uncle Jake said. "It's giving them bad dreams."

"It wasn't a dream!" Sabrina cried.

Daphne entered the hallway, dragging her blanket behind her. She rubbed the sleep from her eyes with her free hand and looked around grumpily. "Can't a person get some shut-eye around here?"

"Sabrina had a bad dream," Granny Relda explained.

"I did not!"

"She says she saw something in the toilet," Uncle Jake said.

"I swear I flushed," Daphne said.

"Ugh! I'll show you!" Sabrina said as she pulled her grandmother into the bathroom. She pointed at the toilet, then took a step back. "It's in there!"

Granny set her battle-ax on the floor and smiled. "Honestly, Sabrina, I think you're a little old to be scared of the boogeyman."

The old woman lifted the toilet lid. There was the little man, rubbing a red knot on the top of his head and glaring at the crowd.

"What's the big idea?" he growled.

Startled, Granny slammed the lid down just as Sabrina had done. Sabrina, Daphne, and even Uncle Jake cried out in fright and backed out of the bathroom.

"Now do you believe me?" Sabrina said.

"Oh, my!" Granny cried. "I'll never doubt you again!"

"What should we do, Mom?" Uncle Jake asked the old woman.

"Elvis!" Granny Relda shouted.

Seconds later an enormous blur of brown fur barreled up the stairs, knocking a few pictures off the wall as it stampeded into the bathroom and came to a screeching halt. Only then could Sabrina see him properly: Elvis, the family's two-hundred-pound Great Dane. He barked at the toilet fiercely, snarling and snapping at the lid.

"Get him, boy!" Daphne ordered.

"You better surrender!" Uncle Jake shouted at the toilet. "Our dog is very hungry!"

Just then, another door opened down the hall and a shaggy-haired boy in cloud-covered pajamas stepped into the hallway.

He scratched his armpit and let out a tremendous belch. "What's all the racket out here?"

"There's something horrible in the toilet!" Daphne shouted.

"Yeah, I think I forgot to flush," Puck said.

"Not that! A little man," Granny Relda said.

"Oh," Puck said. "That's just Seamus."

"And who is Seamus?" Sabrina demanded.

"He's part of your new security detail. Now that Mr. Canis is in jail, the house needs looking after, and to be honest, I'm too busy to do it myself. So I hired you all a team of bodyguards."

"Why is he in the toilet?" Uncle Jake pressed.

"Well, duh! He's guarding it, of course."

"Whatever for?" Granny asked.

"The toilet is a vulnerable entrance into this house," Puck explained. "Anything could crawl up the pipes and take a bite out of your—"

"We get the idea," Granny Relda interrupted. "What are we going to do when we need to use it?"

"Seamus takes regular breaks and has lunch every day at noon," Puck said.

"This is ridiculous," Sabrina said. "We don't need bodyguards and we don't need you to put some freak in the toilet!"

Puck frowned. "You should really watch who you're calling a freak. He's a leprechaun."

Seamus lifted the lid and crawled out of the toilet. He now had two purple lumps on his head and an angry look in his eyes. "I didn't sign on for this abuse, Puck. I quit!"

"Quit? You can't quit," Puck said. "Who will I get to replace you?"

"Go find a toilet elf. What do I care?" the leprechaun shouted as he stomped down the hall and between the legs of Uncle Jake, leaving a trail of little wet footprints behind him.

Puck frowned and turned back to Sabrina. "Now look what you've done—you've made Seamus quit! Do you know how hard it is to find someone to sit in a toilet all night?"

"How many more leprechauns are in the house?" Daphne asked, peering behind the shower curtain.

"That was the only one," Puck said.

"Good!" Sabrina said, relieved.

"But there's about a dozen trolls, some goblins, a few elves and brownies, and a chupacabra staking out the other vulnerable areas of the house."

Sabrina gasped. "There are freaks all over the house?"

"Again, *freak* is a really ugly term. It highlights how ignorant you are. This is the twenty-first century, you know," Puck replied.

Sabrina clenched her fist. "I'm going to highlight your mouth, pal."

To be continued . . .

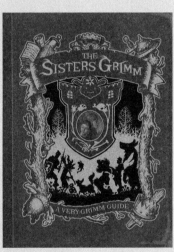